AH BAO AND THE
FOX PRINCESS

By Mick Kilburn
Copyright held by Mick Kilburn 2019
First Edition Apeil 13, 2021

Foreword

The stories of foxes and princesses with foxlike spirits have per-meated Chinese culture, and other cultures, as well, for thousands of years. The fox is an object that represents fertility and fecundity. This story of Ah Bao is a little different from those you may have read. Ah Bao, Chang Wen Ming, comes from a family of fishermen, and though he too is a fisherman, and has a boat to fish with, passed down to him from his father, lately his nets have been empty.

Ah Bao lives during the precarious time in China at the beginning of the 20th Century. He's lost both of his parents, as other families have, to influenza. His best friend and neighbor, Xin Jun, is away in the North, fighting for the Southern War Lords alongside the Boxers. Add to these uncertainties, Ah Bao has noticed something strange happening to his boat.

Ah Bao and the Fox Princess

We can hear the sound of a flute playing like in an old Chinese Opera, as a general stops, and slowly, crisply, goes through his machinations.

Chang Wen Ming, known to his friends as Ah Bao, stood in the pre-dawn darkness
in his mountain cottage, in the small village, of Jinhuazhen, outside the city of Luoyang. The dampness in the Summer dawn air was oppressive, like a cool, moist blanket covering him and, everything in the room. Ah Bao woke, as every morning since his parents had died, extracted the last wooden match from a small matchbox, and knowing it was the last one, struck it carefully against the matchbox.

As if to prevent its own demise the damp match, softened by the dampness, rubbed unresisting against the matchbox, and as Ah Bao half expected, failed to light. Ah Bao tried again, this time striking it more quickly, the match beginning to ignite, though only for a moment, producing the briefest of bright, wet sputters. Hoping to keep the tip from crumbling apart in his fingers, Ah Bao turned the match to the opposite side of the matchhead, and again dragged it carefully across an unblemished place on the rough strip attached to the side of the matchbox. In the darkness, a miracle, a tiny yellow and white spark began at the head of the match, at first almost listlessly, then ignited the tip of the match into a tenuous flame, slowly revealing to him in a dull ocher light the whitewashed walls of the small cottage room.

The light from the wooden match fell on objects in the room that were familiar to Ah Bao. The earthen kang, beside the wooden table where he ate his meals, the wooden benches on each side of the table, the iron cook stove against one wall, and the wooden three-legged stool between it and the table. Each of these objects, if he'd wanted to, he could have easily found in the dark. The light from the match, itself, was unnecessary for what he needed to do. Only the flame, the necessary element he needed to perform his predawn ritual. Ah Bao put the matchbox down quickly, as he reached for the bundle of incense, which he could see laying on the wide, polished earthen windowsill next to where he stood. Not picking it up, with his left hand carefully withdrawing two long thin sticks from within the crisp, deep crimson-colored paper. As he freed the incense sticks, withdrawing them slowly from the tightly wrapped incense packet, the fine incense powder brushed off onto the paper, filling the air around Ah Bao with the pleasing scent of sandalwood. Lighting the ends of the two sticks of incense, with the match, he let the match's flame sit for a long moment under the tips of the incense, until the ends of the incense began to glow. He blew lightly on the incense sticks, the ends glowing a brighter red, then the tips yellow hot.

But the glowing yellow embers of the incense made Ah Bao a little melancholy, and he thought, at that moment, the only way he thought he might raise his spirits, to rid his mind of a brief sadness, was to recite to himself the haiku, many days before that had formed in his mind. As he inhaled the sweet sandalwood smoke from the incense, he thought for a long moment:

Loved Ones that are Gone,
Remembering with incense,
As the sweetness fades.

The light was unnecessary for Ah Bao to complete his predawn task, which he felt in his heart he must do throughout the past year, and as he performed the ritual this morning, he allowed himself to be momentarily be captivated by the thought of his haiku. He permitted himself to dwell for only a moment on the haiku, that at the same time somehow showed to him the yin and yang of life and death, both embodied in the flame of the burning, wooden match and the incense. The yang of death was certainly the flame's consuming fire. The warmth he felt from the heat of the burning wood on his cool fingertips, his senses told him, must embody the yin of birth, of life. Each aspect of the flame a continuation, and at the same time arising from the other complimentary aspect.

The fire of the flame, and the warmth of the wooden match both he knew must end, as would the sweet scent of the incense would eventually fade. The thought, that sensation, he began that day with, thinking about his parents, and praying for their spirits to be at peace. Trying to remember their presence, and honoring their memories.

Having lit the incense, Ah Bao turned slowly, blowing once more on the lit incense, to making sure the ends were lit, and gazed directly into the faces of his parents; into the stern, unquestioning eyes of his father, and the serious, melancholy eyes of his mother. Their faces were framed in two black draped photos, displayed on the long, polished, pine table, against the sandstone cottage wall of the living room, facing toward the door that opened toward the West. Ah Bao looked deep into his mother's lovely eyes, fuller, and rounder, than those of the Han families, who recently had moved into the valley from the north, to live, and fill the village, and the city of Luoyang with their houses and their businesses.

His mother's eyes were almond shaped, as were Ah Bao's, the rounder almond shape of the local Henan people who had lived in these mountains, and on these rivers of Henan province, as long as history could recall. The fullness, the roundness of his mother's eyes, though now, in the photograph only added to her look of melancholy.

Ah Bao easily recalled the day the photos had been taken. The traveling photographer had come to the front of their cottage, his back stooped from carrying his bulky, shiny wooden box camera, on top its long iron tripod. And though moments before the photographs were taken, his mother had been smiling, resting her loving hand on Ah Bao's shoulder, standing, waiting in the shade of a tall persimmon tree, behind the cottage. As the photographer set up his camera, and positioned Mr. Chang, Ah Bao's father, to be photographed, his mother looked at her husband sitting in front of the camera, and the set of his mother's eyes slowly took on the serious, anxious, melancholy look she had in the photograph. as if expecting something, and now gazing back at him. Ah Bao wondered if she had somehow divined her and her husband's untimely death.

The match in Ah Bao's fingers rapidly reached its end and Ah Bao blowing on it lightly, extinguished it, and was once again standing alone with his thoughts in the gray-black darkness of the approaching dawn. But Ah Bao was not a young man, perhaps close to thirty, and he wasn't one to wallow in self-pity, even though his sad, lonely conditions might provide the fuel for a younger, weaker man who might fall into despair, he had already reached thirty, and his mother had instilled in him as he was growing up to accept his life as it was, while at the same time, making the best of what he would struggle against, whatever the obstacles that might present themselves to him.

But as a younger man he had gotten kicked in the head by a horse he was standing behind, he had been helping to shoe, that left a thin half-moon crescent from the horse's hoof across his forehead, close to his hairline. He had a flowerpot fall on his head, and been knocked him senseless for a few minutes, the one side effect, perhaps, being of late he'd begun to ponder life, and other natural phenomena.

And yet, this morning as Ah Bao pondered the yin and yang of the flame of the burning match, and he told himself, assured himself, had he not been a poor man, as he was now, with almost no money at all, he would have been more generous in his filial devotion, and used six sticks of incense; three each, for his mother and his father, a much more fortuitous number.

Ah Bao loved and worshiped his parents, who had meant more to him than anything, and their memory now held an equally treasured place in his mind. He felt that if he had three sticks of incense for each of his parents, not only a much more auspicious number, the more generous amount would have shown much more filial love, certainly, than a paltry single stick of incense for each of his parents. But Ah Bao's pockets were empty of silver, only a few coppers, hardly enough to buy a little rice, let alone more incense, and he tried not to waste much thought on what might have been, knowing he should be satisfied he had at least had one stick of incense for each of his parents, even though it was the least expensive variety of sandalwood incense sold in the market. There were others villagers, he told himself, he warned himself, who had far less.

CHAPTER TWO

In the half darkness of the dawning Ah Bao placed the two sticks of incense between his hands, blew lightly, gently on the glowing tips fanning the embers, and raised his hands above his forehead, praying slowly, bowing, slowly, three times in succession to each of the photographs, of his parents, first his father, and then his mother. Then once again standing facing the photographs of his parents, he took one of each of the sticks of incense and pressed the unlit end upright, firmly into the small bowls of sand in front of each of the framed images, and since he'd caught no fish, he had no money to buy enough rice to place the incense sticks in.

Just as he didn't need the light from the flame of the match to find his way around the room, Ah Bao didn't need the brief few moments of light to perform his prayers, his supplications to his parents. Yet, he forced himself to focus on both his thoughts, and his movements, which were worn into his mind, and added the thought of his haiku, making his thoughts of devotion stronger. He had been expressing his love and devotion, in the predawn darkness, for most of the past year, and after a year he had begun to feel like he was performing his prayers in his sleep.

He wished though that there was something more he could do to honor his parents, and somehow be assured that he had allowed their spirits to rest in peace. If someone were to ask him, and he had been allowed to voice his deepest feelings, Ah Bao knew that he would have said there was nothing he would not undertake to honor the memories of his father and his mother, to bring them the peace he knew they sought in the afterlife.

And at the beginning of that lunar month, it had been one year since he had lost both his parents, and that week, those tragic days seemed like only yesterday. The memory of the rapid turn of events was still so fresh in his mind, that recalling it was like staring into a white-hot flame, and too much for his mind to bear. What made it even harder for him, as he woke, and stood in the predawn darkness of the cottage each morning, was realizing as he stirred himself from sleep to perform his filial ritual, was that what he wanted to believe was a nightmarish dream, from which he might soon awake, he knew would never end, and the loneliness, and the loss he felt, ached like a hole in the center of his spirit.

This morning, as with each morning, as Ah Bao lit the incense, bowed to his parents' photographs, said his prayers, and expressed the only tangible way he felt he could show his feelings of filial piety, a tiny glimmer of sunlight began to filter through the southern window of the small cottage. Although most of the morning sunlight was caught, and filtered, by the dense stand of bamboo long ago, which one of his ancestors had planted a few yards between the front of the cottage and the road, to keep the cottage cooler during these humid summer months.

The thick bamboo was meant to trap the clouds of rising dust, as well, from the traffic of oxen and wagons, on autumn market days, on the road that ran in front of his family's cottage and snaked on into the village. Though some of the bamboo was no bigger around than fat blades of tall grass, some of the shiny, emerald-green bamboo poles were as large around as a man's thigh. On the other side of the road were the tops of tall silver white-barked pine trees growing on the rolling hill that sloped steeply down toward the river.

This morning, like every morning, as Ah Bao saw the sunlight from the East, peeking through the rippled and discolored windowpanes of the Southern window, the glass coated and stained with countless years of wood smoke and cooking grease, the light roused him from his thoughts, and he turned and took the three short steps back to the broad brick and earthen kang, where he slept each night.

He sat down on the edge of the cotton quilt covering the still warm kang, and slowly rubbed the sleep from his eyes with one hand, and scratched the back of his neck with the other. He ran his fingers through his tangled hair, and slowly began combing his long, black hair, before starting the tedious process of braiding it into the long queue which fell from the back of his head, and down the middle of his back.

Since the founding of the Republic, with the queue laws being rescinded, many of the other young men in the village, and throughout China, had been cutting off their queues, though Ah Bao had resolutely vowed to keep his. The old edict passed by the Qing emperors hundreds of years before warning that either "lose your hair and keep your head, or keep your hair and lose your head," meaning if young men didn't shave the front of their heads Manchu style, though able to keep the rest of their hair in long queues, they would be beheaded. With the fall of Emperor Qian Long and the establishment of the Republic of China, the edict was no longer applied, and though the reason for Ah Bao keeping his queue was more than simply his wanting to flaunt the now toothless edict, he had decided the reason for not cutting his long queue was with all that had changed, losing his parents, and now for so long not being able to catch fish, it was one of the few things he could do to try to keep things from changing even further.

Ah Bao had read very few books, and though he was semiliterate, he didn't keep any books in the cottage, nor had his parents before him. That wasn't true for the next-door neighbor girl, Lu Mei Rong, or Mei Mei, as everyone called her, the younger sister of Lu Xin Jun, Ah Bao's closest friend from childhood, their families being men dang hu dui, living opposite doors on the road above the river, the two households alike in their family positions. Ah Bao's family had owned a large boat for generations, and were fishermen, while Lu Mei Rong's father, Lu Xin Fang, sold cereals, and other grains, in a shop in the city of Luoyang, and although books were hard to find, and expensive, Mei Mei read from the annals that her father had purchased with money earned from the sale of his hardware. Mei Mei would also find ways to borrow others things to read that were hard to find. She was uncharacteristic for a girl of her time, an avid reader of not only books, but whatever written word she might encounter, whether it might be old inserts for medicine, or old journals, or tattered sheets of ancient scripture.

As they had grown up together, Xin Jun, and Ah Bao, might be walking along, Mei Rong, following them, a few steps behind, talking incessantly, quoting whatever her new found knowledge acquired from her books, a constant, almost unending commentary on what she'd learned. They mostly ignored her, talking or wrestling together, as they began to grow and fill out, no longer tender boys, almost the same size, equal adversaries.

But it had been in the Spring of that, the seventh year of the founding of the new Republic, and Mei Mei had told Ah Bao about a book she had been reading, the Confucian Classic of Filial Piety. She had found a copy of it lying among the dusty stacks of books in the rear of the White Horse temple. The Buddhist temple was not far from their village, and she had borrowed it without question from one of the old monks.
The Classic stated, she had said loudly, with an elbow to Ah Bao's ribs to make sure she had his attention, that "one should keep and not damage the body, the hair and the skin."

She said this explained the reason Chinese men didn't want to cut their hair, on the front of their heads, in the first place, and why they had resisted the Manchu queue laws when they began as far back in the seventeen Century.

With the new laws of the Republic, and rapidly changing ways, many young people had abandoned the old ways, and were now moving from the villages into the cities. But Ah Bao felt that Jinhuazhen, his village, that got its name on the land where it sat and pressed out into the river where it sat, was his home, his ancestral home, and the one lasting tie he still had with his parents, and Ah Bao assured himself, and in turn, Mei Mei, he would not be joining the other young men across China in their flight to find more opportunity in the provincial capitals, discarding their conservative provincial ways for what everyone knew was a looser, easier city life. His resolve was bolstered, as well, by the fact that keeping a queue, as Mei Mei had plainly stated, according to the classics, was an overt expression of filial piety, and in remembrance of his parents, for that reason he swore to himself to not cut his.

CHAPTER THREE

Once Ah Bao had finished braiding his queue, and flipped it over his back like a long shiny black horse's tail, he squatted over the chamber-pot which sat behind the kang, and emptied his body of its dirt, and his bladder of its water. Standing, he stepped off the chamber pot, and let his nightshirt fall back down over his legs. Turning he reached across the thick quilt, embroidered with large, lovely red peonies, and longnecked red-headed storks. The bright cotton quilt which lay covering the still warm kang, the warmth of the quilt still radiating heat, as he reached across to where his clothes hung against the headboard of the kang, was calling him back to sleep,. He forced himself to stand up and began to quickly dress.

As he pulled on his light cotton shirt his mood began to change, and he allowed himself to recall some of the happier days he had shared with his parents, and the better times they had together. The village of Jinhuazhen sat along a curve in the river, and the Changs never seem to go hungry, since each season there were different fish in the river to catch. Ah Bao's father had been famous among the other fishermen in Jinhuazhen for his ability to somehow always draw fish into his net.

Ah Bao thought about how he and his father would go fishing each day on the river, either rowing up to a particular bend in the river, or drifting down the river and anchor next to a shoal. His father knew just where to set the nets, and they would return to the beach their nets often bulging with fat, silvery carp, and long meaty catfish. They would almost always catch more than enough fish for the three of them to eat, and have some left over to sell on the beach, or trade for fishing supplies in Luoyang. Ah Bao sat on the edge of the cold kang, where his parents had slept until the day of their deaths, and he had slept in a rope cot in front of the kang, the warmth of the heat of the wood in the firebox, while he and his father fished, his mother filled with wood she gathered each day from beneath the pine and birch trees in the forest. After their deaths, Ah Bao had taken to sleeping in his parents' place on the wide kang, and even on cold winter days often letting it grow cold, making him stiff and dreamless when he would awake. Most days he was too tired after laying and gathering the net alone, to go back down the hill and gather firewood.

Ah Bao sat lost in thought as he slowly pulled on the thick, dark, patched cotton pants that hung next to the thick, quilted, cotton mian ao, he wore to stay warm on chilly winter days. He recalled how, during those once cheerful times on cold mornings, his mother might have already been heating for him and his father a breakfast of thick geng, with pieces of salted fish, and pungent mushrooms. Or, how on special mornings, those special days on the temple calendar that his mother would have observed, and would have been preparing a pot of rice congee, xi fan. And on special holidays she might prepare a babaofan, with all the eight treasures in the rice; the sweet rice mixed with tender peanuts, and red dates and longyan, and a small handful of lotus seed purchased from the dry goods store, boiled with goji berries., and the pine nuts she had gathered, and yellow raisins she would pick from the vine beside the cottage.

Occasionally, around the New Year, she might find a silver wood fungus, on a fallen tree somewhere along the hill, when she was out gathering firewood, and she would add that to the rice, completing the babaofan.

Once Ah Bao had finished combing his hair, and dressing, he picked up the clay chamber-pot, and walked out through the back door of the cottage into the backyard. As he walked through the tall grass beyond the back of the house, beside where he drew his water from the well each morning, his pet dog, Wei Wei, stretched from his place in the doorway of his own small, bamboo, doghouse beside the persimmon tree.

This morning, as each morning, Wei Wei greeted Ah Bao barking, not once, but twice, his morning greeting, his hello. That was the reason Ah Bao had named him Wei Wei, as a pup, more than five years before. The dog joined Ah Bao, falling in beside him, as he walked on out of the backyard, toward a stand of trees, where a shallow, grassy, drainage ditch ran diagonally away behind his cottage, toward the rear of the other nearby cottages, as the hillside followed the river, descending gradually as it flowed East. Here is where Ah Bao dumped his chamber-pot, letting the clay pot rest at an angle face down on the grass for a moment, allowing all its contents run into the ditch.

Ah Bao left the chamber-pot at the side of the ditch, and walked back up to the well. Wei Wei sat down at Ah Bao's feet looking up at him as he drew a half full bucket of water from the well. He sat the bucket on the brick edge of the well, and splashed the cool well water onto his face and hands, enjoying the water as it invigorated him. Looking down at his dog, he noticed how Wei Wei was growing a little thinner, his ribs showing distinctively along his sides, he too mourning the passing of Ah Bao's parents, not savoring, for more than a year, the tasty scraps Ah Bao's mother had regularly tossed out the back door to him, while she had been alive.

Ah Bao walked back toward the house, through the open doorway, and sat down at the long, polished wooden table, which sat in the middle of the room, where he and his parents had taken their meals each day. Sitting down on one of the well worn pine benches that surrounded the table, he thought about how during earlier, happier times his father, had always risen, dressed and washed, and woken Ah Bao from his sleep, and would probably by now be quickly finished eating his breakfast, and already be beginning his preparation to leave for the morning fishing.

Ah Bao had traded with a qianpu, a stringer of coppers, the one fish he'd caught a few days before for two string of ten coppers. and he unwrapped and took from the oiled cloth that sat on a small, flat, faded blue, ceramic plate, in the center of the table, the two cold, steamed buns which he had purchased the evening before from a baker at the edge of the village, using one of the small strings of coppers. The other small chuan of copper coins sat next to the blue plate in the middle of the table. He had decided he'd use the last small chuan for two more buns if he was again unable to catch fish.

One of the buns was a cheap plain one, though he allowed himself the luxury of buying the other one stuffed with sweet red bean paste. Although Ah Bao was ravenously hungry, and could have swallowed both buns in a few gulping bites, he waited and slowly peeled the dried skin that had formed on the outside of the buns, and lay the skin on the table next to the plate. Which he'd later feed to Wei Wei.

Ah Bao took a bite of the plain bun, and as he began to chew it, the water began to form in his mouth, and he slowly swallowed it, and it began to ease the gnawing hunger in the pit of his stomach. When he began to eat the second, sweet, stuffed bun, savoring the red bean paste at its center, it allowed his mind to return to the many days he had spent on the river with his father, catching the fish, and selling them to villagers that came down to the beach, always knowing the Chang boat would have fish.

He thought about their small wooden boat, with it's tiny canvas sail, and how he and his father took turns relieving each other at the rudder, or at the oars, as they rowed the boat up the river, against the currents, laying one end of the net in a sheltered cove, then riding the swiftly moving currents floating rapidly back down the river, past submerged rocks and fallen trees jutting into the river, to drop the other end, careful not to allow the net to get caught.

His father showed Ah Bao secret places along the river where only he knew the largest fish would often be lurking. He cautioned Ah Bao that he would only lay his net in those stretch of the river when there were no other boats around, not wanting to give away his secret spots. Ah Bao thought how he wished that he had watched and listened more closely to his father's instructions. But he had naively assumed that he would have his father, as the years wore on, even as the older man became to old to pull against the oars, and he would simply ride along in the boat and continue to instruct Ah Bao.

Even after several years at his father's side Ah Bao was still not half the fisherman that his father had been. He lacked the understanding of the waters of the river and the subtleties of fishing that might only come with age, and time. There were days when gusts of wind were blowing heavily across the river, or there had been several days of torrential rains further up the river, his father had shown Ah Bao how to handle the boat safely in the churning eddies, and unpredictable currents along the more rocky, rapid, treacherous parts of the river. Once he had gotten older, when he had occasionally been allowed to accompany his father, during those more dangerous days on the river, when the weather was too fresh, the wind blowing harder, he had always felt so safe beside him in the boat no matter what the conditions.

And then, shortly after the Lunar New Year celebration things had all happened so suddenly. Who could have known that fortune would play such a fateful trick on their family. His mother had judiciously consulted the calendar, and the forces of ming, the powers that governed fate, and during those auspicious days, found they coincided with cai and fu, the forces that governed finances and wealth, and she decided on a day for her husband to travel.

His father too had felt it had been a propitious time to purchase a new fishing net. He had gotten two gaping holes on the rocks in the old net too large to mend, the webbing in the old net with age, breaking more easily. There were other supplies he needed to purchase: lead weights, corks, and a long, thick, length of rope needed to replace the worn one tied to the boat's anchor. His father decided that it was a good time to make the trip to Hong Kong where he knew some of the shops used the best line to weave their fishing nets. In the city the best cork, line, and lead could be purchased for the best price, too.

CHAPTER FOUR

On the fifteen day after the Lunar New Year the family, along with the families in the rest of the village, had celebrated the traditional Lantern Festival. Ah Bao's mother had prepared glutinous rice balls stuffed with sesame butter, and they visited the temple, and prayed and burnt incense in offerings for a safe and expeditious trip. On the way back to their home the three of them as was often the tradition had played guess the riddle, and Ah Bao had been especially clever solving riddles written on several lanterns hanging from the shop fronts in the village along the way, and Ah Bao had felt carefree as they laughed and joked during the walk back. It was the end of the New Year's celebrations and Ah Bao's father had felt it was truly an auspicious time to make a trip.

That night his mother had packed a small suitcase for his father with a change of clothes and some dried fish, peanuts, and a packet of dried noodles to boil once he boarded the train. Late the following day, full of optimism and purpose his father accompanied by Ah Bao and his mother had walked to the village, Ah Bao dutifully carrying his father's suitcase, to the tiny building that served as a train station at the far end of the line of shops that was the main street through the village. They had waited a short while until they could hear the approaching train and quickly said their goodbyes. The train pulled into the village, hardly stopping, only long enough to offload a few packages, and allow Ah Bao's father to show the conductor his ticket and climb aboard. In several large black billows of smoke the train had lurched forward and begun moving again and pulled through and out of the town headed south.

Ah Bao's father had taken the overnight train south from their village of Jinhuazhen, in Szechuan, to Hong Kong. If perhaps his father had been reading the newspaper during the weeks leading up to his trip, he would have seen the articles written in lurid details, and probably would not have taken the trip at that time, and it could all have been prevented. But his father found little time to read, felt that the cost of a newspaper was a waste of money, and felt that the most prudent use for old newspapers that passed through his hands were to wrap the fish in that he traded and sold in the village.

And so his father had not known about the influenza which had begun to rage weeks before in Hong Kong. Through the night the train had carried him south through Guiyang and Guangzhou, finally arriving late the following day at its destination. He had boiled his noodles and eaten his fish during the trip in preparation for his excursion to the bustling, frenetic city of Hong Kong. When he had stepped off of the train at its destination in the Kowloon train station late that afternoon he had been unaware of what awaited him in the port city. He had only been aware of the discomfort of the beating sheets of icy rain, long curtains of water, the wind blowing them almost horizontal as they soaked passersby and flooded the streets.

He had taken the ferry across the bay to Wanchai where he could purchase his supplies, and only stayed for one night as planned in Hong Kong, the cost of a room an added expense he was forced to tack on to the expenditures for his fishing supplies. Although that night as he lay down to sleep, after hanging his soaking clothes up in the tiny cramped stuffy little room in hopes that they could dry, he sensed something was wrong. And yet, the following morning he immediately realizing from the panic which seized the city, that what he had originally thought was a fortuitous time following the Lunar New Year's celebrations to make a trip and purchase a new fishing net, had been a dire mistake. He had hurriedly purchased the net, lead weights, and other necessary supplies, and as he made his way through the streets again was soaked by the pelting rain, his one set of dry clothes now also drenched. Everywhere throughout the city, including the shoddy three story hotel where he was staying, occupants were gripped by racking coughs, and the malaise of influenza. He returned quickly to his hotel room gathered together his belongings and his purchases and made his way to the train station. He slept exhausted atop his bag and his purchases until the next train arrived late that day heading back north to Szechuan.

CHAPTER FIVE

Ah Bao finished his breakfast and poured himself a cup of cold tea brewed the night before, and taking a sip the smoky, pu er flavor of the tea cleansing his mouth. He picked up the tea cup and a leather covered volume of verse and carried those things out into the dawn to greet the sun. Ah Bao loved everything about nature. He loved the rivers and the fish. He loved the mountains and trees that surrounded his village, and he loved the stones and clay mud from which his house had been built more than a century before.

Ah Bao's parents had been devout Buddhists and for that reason wishing to be a good filial son practiced religiously all the rituals that this entailed. He took these practices seriously paying close attention to the details governing the observance of these rituals, burning the burial paper during the prescribed holy days to provide money for the spirits of his parents wherever they might be, and put out what little food he could afford as offerings in the temple. At the same time he was spiritually drawn by his love of nature to the other temple, the Taoist temple, and the Taoist beliefs that the mysterious ways of nature and the earth are sacred. He had only begun exploring these tenets in the Dao De Jing, within the leather bound book he carried since his parent's death, but the passages which he stumbled over each morning as the sun began to rise in the sky, though often not revealing answers to him, and frequently mystifying him even more than he was before reading them, in thought and meditation led him to a place of peace away from the hollow emptiness bordering on despair he had been feeling since the loss of his parents.

When his parents were alive he would never have dared to purchase a book of Taoist scripture, let alone any book, and yet he hadn't. It had been on a morning like this no long after his parent's death and he had come out to sit on the stone bench under the gnarled, old stone pine tree which sat nestled against the corner of the wall that surrounded his house, and where his father used to sit in the evenings and mend his net. Ah Bao had been sipping his cold tea looking out through the open gate watching the sunrise through the bamboo and the pine when a passing monk had stopped, seen Ah Bao sitting alone, bowed and asked if he might enter. Ah Bao had invited him in and sitting together on the stone bench the old monk had talked with the young man for a short while.

The old monk's chocolate colored robes though old and almost threadbare were immaculately clean as was the peaked hat that he wore. And although Ah Bao couldn't guess the monk's age his face was heavily lined with wrinkles which almost reached back and touched his ears when the old man smiled. His hands were gnarled and the color of chestnut and when he placed one of his hands on Ah Bao's shoulder to reassure him he could feel the strength within it.

Ah Bao wasn't able to recall exactly what he and the old monk had talked about that first day besides the obvious sadness Ah Bao was feeling from the loss of his parents, but before leaving the monk had placed in the younger man's hands the small leather bound copy of the Taoist Scriptures, saying he wanted to lend Ah Bao the book, it might provide him a bit of guidance, and that the monk would be back at a later time to retrieved it. He had also mentioned that perhaps he would instruct Ah Bao in the practice of tai chi, a way of moving meditation which Ah Bao might use to invigorate his body and raise his spirits when overcome by his grief.

And yet it had been almost a year now, and the monk had not returned, though Ah Bao knew he lived not far away at the nearby Jinhua Temple, the Taoist temple for which his village, Jinhuazhen had been named. Once, several months earlier, Ah Bao had made the long walk to the temple to seek out the old monk and found only a young boy of about twelve sweeping the stone steps that led up to the temple to where it sat nestled in the pines on a large knoll. The boy had told Ah Bao that all the monks were traveling and he wasn't sure exactly when they might return.

Ah Bao having hoped to locate the monk and speak with him, returned home temporarily dejected. Ah Bao eagerly anticipated the old monk's return and looked forward to the talks that they might have about the book, hoping he might be able to elucidate some of the passages for him, he was also apprehensive at having to part with the book. Still, Ah Bao did feel a little like he was ignoring his parents own beliefs, which they had done their best to try to instill in him, by only worshiping briefly each morning in front of their photos, then coming out into the rising sun, reading a short passage of the Taoist scriptures, and then reveling at length in the mysterious beauty around him. And yet this practices allowed him to hold his life together. He knew too that Buddhism and Taoism, and even Confucian beliefs had existed and complimented each of the others for thousands of years. His Confucian beliefs provided him with a model for a positive attitude, the Buddhist laws provided him with the thought of an afterlife and peace, and the Taoist doctrine allowed him to retreat and meditate on nature and the world around him.

This was not to say there had not been isolated moments during those preceding months when he had felt so alone and grief ridden that he had trouble finding any reason to continue living. There had been long stretches of days when he caught no fish, his pockets were empty, and he had very little food to survive on. If it hadn't been for the constant reminder of the life his hardworking parents had lived and most especially the thought which his mother's spirit provided him, that he must continue with his life, overcome all the obstacles that were placed in his path, and do his best to carry on, he might not have been able to continue with his life. And yet, over time, with the bit of little earthly guidance the old Taoist monk had given Ah Bao, and his continued struggle to read and understand the scriptures, he had found and was beginning to feel some of the optimism that he knew his father had always possessed, and perhaps as his parents had undoubtedly hoped for him, sometime in the future he might find someone to share his life with and carry on his family line.

At other times, slowly sipping his tea, lost in thought, Ah Bao would run his hand along the edge of the stone bench polished smooth through the years where his father, and his father before him had rested their arms countless times when mending nets. Ah Bao would watch the birds, the nuthatches darting back and forth from the line of pine trees outside his gate, first landing on the wall, and then darting into the stone pine tree above his head, singing gaily as they picked at the pine cones and the pine nuts locked inside them that filled the tree's branches. After some time, sitting in solitude his thoughts moving from one thing to another, some mornings, like today, he would invariably begin to think about the loss of his parents, tears would fill his eyes, and he would sit weeping silently, the tears running down his cheeks.

If one were to meet Ah Bao, not knowing his heart or the mind of the young man, from outward appearance one would never have thought he an overly sensitive young man. His parents had taught him, and shown by example, that it was imprudent to display one's emotions, and if or when he did, it would most often be taken by others as a sign of a weakness in his character. Although Ah Bao had spent a few short years in the village school learning to read and write, once he had grown old enough to help his father in the boat, he had left school and begun to work side by side with him, fishing each day. Ah Bao possessed a strong lean body which had been tempered, working beside his father, laying out, setting the net as his father guided him, then hauling the fishing net in a short while later, often times bristling with the flashing silver and golden sides of the rivers fish. He would do this hour after hour, as he worked hand over hand, until the muscles in his back would burn with the effort. And though Ah Bao, lacking the expertise his father had possessed at reading the river and the hiding places of the schools of fish, and had grown a great deal thinner, just as his dog Wei Wei had, without the motherly attention he missed, he still possessed a strong and supple body, and he still forced himself out on to the river each day fishing as he tried to fill his net.

CHAPTER SIX

In addition to a strong and well toned body, Ah Bao had managed to retain the openhearted benevolent spirit nurtured by the kindness his mother had shown him, and by her own model of self-sacrifice. As he was growing up the woman had been an example of both empathy and selflessness for the boy, teaching him what it meant to care for others and put those that one loved before one's own comfort or satisfaction. She had always filled her own bowl last after she had seen that the men had enough to eat, and she was always the last one to go to bed, after the last of the household chores had been completed. But it had been this expression of self-sacrifice in her final days which at times brought Ah Bao close to the brink of despair.

On the day his father returned from his trip to Hong Kong Ah Bao was waiting at the train station in Jinhuazhen. The older man complained of an aching discomfort and had begun to cough. Ah Bao carried his bag and walked arm and arm with him his father resting against him as they walked. When they reached home, his wife made him tea and he fell into bed on the kang trying to rest. By nightfall, though, he was racked by an endless phlegm filled hacking, and unable to sleep. Ah Bao's mother tended her husband throughout the night, warming tea, and placing cool compresses on his now fevered body.

Then, by the next day his mother had begun coughing terribly, and though his father appeared to have improved slightly with his mother's tending, he remained in bed. By the night of the second day both of his parents were bedridden, their coughing and fevers driving Ah Bao to his wits end not knowing what to do or how to help them. Ah Bao had raced to the village herbalist, purchased expensive herbs, and boiled them down to a dark bitter tea for his parents to drink. And yet, throughout the third day both of his parents worsened. Although the room was filled with a clammy, cold, dampness, the quilt which the couple lay beneath also damp with their fevered perspiration. By the night of the third day his mother's lungs filled with a crimson suffocating foam, during the following early morning hours, holding her son's hand, she died.

For some reason the influenza had not affected Ah Bao, although over the next day, as his father continued to worse, his frantic effort to try and ease his father's racking, mucous filled cough, were all but useless. Two days after his mother died Ah Bao's father at about the same time his mother had died, struggling to breathe, his face turning a pale, cyanotic blue, coughing his last breath, had died, as well.

Sitting, warming himself in the morning sun, tears rolling down his face, Ah Bao lay down his tea cup, clasped his hands once again in supplication, and prayed silently that his parents' spirits had been released from their suffering. As he recalled those days of panic and pandemic, during which the village had prohibited all but the briefest of funerals for the dead, and his parents had been quickly buried, Ah Bao felt certain that it had not been enough. He wondered, perhaps that the priest who had come to practice wuyi, of half magic and medicine, waving his wooden sword taped with paper scriptures, and filling the house with the gray, choking clouds of moxi smoke, lighting fireworks, and banging drums and gongs, to drive the spirits of his parents to their resting place, had not had time to work his effects, and either his mother or his father, or both, could still be roaming the area around the house, or the nearby village unable to rest.

During the days immediately following his parents death, although his grief prevented him from consciously realizing it, it was a time when Ah Bao most needed companionship and solace from a friend. Yet during those days because of the fear that gripped the village, and in fact by then because of the pandemic that raged across China and the entire civilized world, he was ostracized by the villagers, and was left almost entirely to his own devices to grieve and try to continue his life. The Lu family, who lived in the house next to the Changs and had been his parent's closest friends, had not failed completely, though from afar, to look after him.

In fact, Lu Xin Jun, the Lu's son had always been Ah Bao's closest childhood friend, and as boys they had done everything together. In their years at school they sat at the same desk reading from the same primer. They did their homework together beside the oil lamp either in the Lus,' or the Changs' cottage, and they consoled each other after the occasional schoolmaster's scolding. They had grown into young men together, but now when Ah Bao needed him most, Xin Jun was no longer beside him to be his friend.

CHAPTER SEVEN

Following the New Year's celebration two years earlier, Xin Jun had decided to join the Army, and unlike Ah Bao's father's choice to travel South to Hong Kong the previous year, for Xin Jun it had been, an auspicious choice, leaving earlier,and only going as far south as Guangzhou, and well before the beginning of the New Year.

Since the Revolution, with the founding of the Republic, and Yuan Shi Kai, or Yan Da Tou, Yan "big head," as people called him, self appointed President from 1912 through 1915, and declaring himself "Great Emperor of China," taking control in 1916, there had been a surge in nationalism throughout the country. And though Yuan had died shortly after making himself emperor, Xin Jun convinced himself he would follow in Da Tou's footsteps, and make a name for himself in the Army.

In letters to his parents Xin Jun had told them he had been promoted once, and had been moved on to the capitol. Though power had splintered among the warlords after Yan Da Tou's death, Xin Jun with the Army had made their way first to Guangzhou, where the'd joined forces with the shadowy, secretive Boxers, and then moved by train North and been stationed in Beiping.

Remaining in the house had been the Lus' daughter, Mei Rong, Mei Mei, who was rather pretty, and though she hadn't lost the plump childish curves she had as an adolescent, she had clean features, and two lovely, shiny braids running down her back. She possessed many of the same attributes of her older brother, Xin Jun, but what Ah Bao found admirable in his young friend, those same traits of strength, steadfastness, and single-mindedness, put him off of the young woman.

CHAPTER EIGHT

It was obvious to everyone that Mei Mei only had eyes for Ah Bao, and she knew she had followed him and her brother around like a puppy when they were younger. And unlike other young women her age who were silent and taciturn, speaking only when spoken to, Mei Mei had trailed after the boys with her nonstop running commentary, in more recent years, though, she had begin to grow a little more distant.

Although the Changs and the Lus had made a silent pact, smiling, and nodding when the children were together, and quite young, a pact that the parents would see Ah Bao and Mei Rong married, and helped to seal the families' friendship, But Ah Bao, through the years, at best, ignored Mei Rong, or simply put up with her. This was undoubtedly the reason in recent years Mei Rong had grown more distant, matching Ah Bao's reticence, becoming a bit more like other young women of a marrying age, playing her mahjong tiles a little more closely to her chest.

But it had been this quality of steadfastness which the young woman still possessed toward Ah Bao, though now more from afar, which had proven during Ah Bao's time of mourning to be the young man's only salvation. During those first weeks after his parents death he would wander aimlessly along the riverbank, sitting for hours staring at the water. At times he watched it as it flowed past, imagining glimpses of his father's face in the rippled reflections, recalling moments when they had been together in their boat on the river. It was almost as if he could hear his father's voice speaking to him above the sound of water as it rushed over the shallower rocky bars reminding him here to steer clear of the shoal. And yet, he didn't have the motivation to take the boat out and go fishing, his spirit drained by his grief. And he told himself that a good filial son would not engage in work, enterprise or endeavor of any kind, when he should be in mourning. At the end of each day, as the sun began to set, dreading the silence of the empty cottage, he would return home empty-handed and hungry.

Ah Bao would once again sit briefly on the stone bench in front of the cottage watching as the night began to engulf him. As the temperature dropped and the cold overtook him he entered the darkening house and would drag himself, physically and mentally drained, to lay down on the kang hopefully finding the refuge of a dreamless sleep. But, many evenings, often as not, he would find a covered plate of dumplings, or noodles, or some rice with a small dish of sauteed vegetables, perhaps still warm, which Mei Mei had brought and silently left in his absence, and which would sustain him for another day. He gratefully accepted the girl's abiding charity, but during those dark days it never crossed his mind even once, as had been the inculcated aspirations of both his and the young woman's parents that eventually he might want to marry Lu Mei Rong. He simply accepted her offerings without any romantic consideration of his own or thinking that there might be any on her part.

As Ah Bao sat in the chilly evening darkness, or occasionally by the light of the sputtering oil lamp, hardly able to buy oil to fill it and to light the room, he had no energy to think about Mei Mei and what a life with her might be like. Instead, he would sit and recall his mother with her small straight-backed frame standing beside her wood burning stove, he standing or seated next to her on the short three legged stool ever present beside the stove on which his mother would sit and peel onions and vegetables. As he recalled their quiet talks, his stomach growling with hunger, it seemed he could almost still taste the delicious sauces of garlic, and soy, and ginger, that she would pour across the sizzling hot fish she scooped from her large iron wok. These thoughts brought him a few moments of solace before his sleep.

And Mei Mei had continued with her acts of kindness, encouraged and prodded by her own mother, and the well worn adage, that a man's heart was through his stomach. Her mother, Mrs. Lu, the extreme opposite of Mrs. Chang, was slightly rotund and unlike the quiet Mrs. Chang went on with a never ending racket of comments and conditions to anyone who would listen, whether in the home, or the village, and probably where Mei Mei had inherited her loose tongue. Mrs. Lu was the wife of a modest rice merchant with a large grain shop in the village who could well afford to allow her daughter to cultivate a field that should mature and produce a husband that would be a substantial provider for her and her children. As of late, though, Mrs. Lu was beginning to wonder if she had perhaps misplaced her confidence in Chang Ah Bao as he faltered in his purpose and his aspirations these last months, and she was beginning to share her concern with her daughter.

And so, there were evenings when Ah Bao would return home having grown almost complacent, half expecting to find something to eat, and there would be nothing. But, then he would reconcile himself to the fact and he would go hungry that night. He didn't consider that perhaps if he had cultivated Mei Rong's interest she might have been more constant in her consideration, and that it was probably only that Mei Rong wanted a little recognition or acknowledgment for her visits, and not really to deprive Ah Bao of his evening meal.

Perhaps to gain this recognition sometimes Mei Rong, and this without Mrs. Lu's encouragement, would mix a little mischief with her altruism. One day she might take all the chopsticks in Ah Bao's house and hide them in a drawer or even under the quilt on the kang. Another evening she might leave them soaking in a bucket outside in a corner of the courtyard. Another time she might leave the meal, especially if it was an particularly fragrant meal, high on a shelf or in at out-of-the-way place where Ah Bao might not expect to look for it, but would finally track it, his belly empty and growling like an animal on the scent for its food. Still another time she would watch and wait from the window of her own cottage where she could see him returning on the path from the river that led up through the woods and then along the front of both buildings. She would allow him time to fall asleep, and then stealth-fully sneak over, and silently leave the meal on the table in the middle of the cottage. Then tiptoeing outside, she make some sort of racket, knocking on the window, or banging a pot to wake him, then scurry home without being seen.

A couple of times when she was bringing over Ah Bao's supper Wei Wei had heard Mei Rong's approaching footsteps, barked, and she had been forced to set the plate down on the stone bench in the courtyard and run away. She had looked into the courtyard the following day, seen the food had been eaten and she could only assume it had been by Ah Bao and not rats or birds. She had taken the plate and returned to her own cottage satisfied that her benevolent act had been appreciated.

But in recent months Mei Rong had become more and more frustrated in her attempts to gain Ah Bao's attention. At the same time, he in his own turn had slowly become less disconsolate in his grieving, and had slowly felt his spirit reawakening within him, his period of mourning having finally reached a degree of closure. In the last weeks on the days when he had begun taking the boat out onto the river, he was beginning to catch a few of the early Spring run of fish which were enough to eat, and to sell in the market and provide him with the cash to buy supplies and other food. He happily continued to eat Mei Rong's offerings in the evening, when she would bring them. But, when Mei Rong would go into Luoyang to help her parents in their grain shop, perhaps at the end of the day she might catch a glimpse of Ah Bao in the village, beside the sprawling wet market in the middle of the city, where other fishermen were selling their fish, and Mei Rong with a slight sense of failure could see that he was now less dependent on her altruism for his survival. Returning and standing behind the counter in her parent's shop, her father in the back with his abacus and ledger, feeling sorry for herself her eyes would begin to well with tears, and she would pull hard on the ends of her twin shiny braids, trying to divert herself from her self pity. It was a trick she had learned from her brother when she was a small girl. When Xin Jun would find Mei Rong sitting and crying for some small reason, Xin Jun would pull on her pigtails, forcing her from her self indulgence, and she would jump up, chase after him, for-getting whatever it had been that had been saddened her. Now though, it only seemed to add fuel to her anger, and Mei Rong's feelings of frustration.

CHAPTER NINE

But Mei Rong was not the only one who had a frustrating situation with which to deal with. Ah Bao had a situation of his own which was beginning to frustrate him, as well. Ever since he was a small boy, and he had learned to swim, his father would take him out onto the river. Along with all the other skills his father had taught him, Mr. Chang had instructed Ah Bao in the importance of the care and maintenance of the boat and the other tools they used, the oars and the net for fishing. It was their livelihood and if something would happen to these things and they were unable to catch fish, as Ah Bao had experienced as of late, he would probably starve. Ah Bao, as he began to take the boat out on the river, now alone for the first time, he followed the habits that his father had taught him to maintain the tools of their trade and never varied, following them religiously, those habits becoming ingrained in his daily routine.

But something truly strange had been occurring in the recent weeks since he had gone back onto the river to fish. Although Ah Bao didn't have a great many years of formal education, he possessed the innate ability to work through the details of most problems and find a solution. But as hard as he tried he could not figure out what was causing this mysterious state of affairs he was now presented with. He had finally settled on the only possible way he was going to solve the mystery, and for the sake of his livelihood he knew it was imperative that he solve the mystery quickly.

It was not that the boat was in need of repair. Mr. Chang had paid constant attention both to the maintenance of his boat and to his nets, and Ah Bao in turn was careful to follow his father's example. Although during his period of mourning Ah Bao had followed the rules of filial piety and not fished, he had taken to heart what his father had taught him in the well worn expression, that a good fisherman didn't spend three days fishing and four days with his nets hanging in the sun. As the old man would often say to him while they worked together on their net or their boat, a fisherman could not afford to waste the days when he should be catching fish on torn nets or a poorly caulked boat, which surely would lead to a dangerously leaking hull.

The mysterious situation was that several times in the last week when carrying his net down to the river, Ah Bao would make his way to where his boat was beached on the riverbank, ready to head out onto the river and go fishing. Each time as he crested the rise of the river bank he could immediately see from a distance that something was out of place. Approaching the boat he could instantly see that the boat lay face up, with the hull against the sand, the oars laying at odd angles on the floor in the bow of the boat. This was not right. There was no question about that. For whatever reason, never on his life would he have left his boat in this condition.

When fishing throughout the day, a fisherman throwing out and retrieving his net, could count on a certain amount of water being hauled into the boat with the fish and dripping net, and could fill the bottom of the boat. In rough weather it was even more severe with the chop from the waves cresting the sides of the boat and splashing aboard. Ah Bao had been taught by his father when returning to the shore to always, without exception, no matter how tired or hurried he might be, to turn the boat over, to drain the water and leave the hull face up so as to allow the sun to dry the wood, and prevent it from becoming waterlogged.

And yet, for some unexplained reason, these several occasions over the past week, the boat had been left in this condition, with the wet hull resting against sand. Someone must be using the boat, and whoever was using it was taking it out at night, or during the early morning hours, and then returning it to the beach this way. But who was the culprit? None of the other fishermen in the village would dare take another man's boat out on to the river without asking, and none had asked him to use his boat. And even if they had taken it without permission, no experienced responsible fisherman, would leave the boat in this condition.

Perhaps it had been some mischievous children, who had rolled the boat over to play in it, fini,shed their games and left it as it was. But if that was the case how did the hull become wet? And Ah Bao couldn't believe that any of the village children would be so audacious, and unless they were almost full grown even have the strength to take the boat out on the river, and as wet as the hull was it was obvious that it had been in the water.

Since all of the fisherman in the village and the neighboring villages recognized each others boats and would have immediately been suspicious if they had seen a stranger in another fisherman's boat, this didn't provide any answers. The least plausible answer to the mystery was that a stranger was taking the boat out at night, but what possible reason would anyone have for taking the boat out at night? And someone, during recent nights, was obviously taking his boat out surreptitiously and returning it to the same place where he beached it and had managed to avoid detection by any suspicious eyes.

As the sun began to rise further in the sky, Ah Bao quickly drained his teacup, slowly got up, gathered up his fishing net from where it hung draped, drying on the rock wall, slung the net over his shoulder, and began the short walk from his house down to the river's edge. He usually wouldn't have left so early to go fishing but he had business to attend to. He wasn't sure if he could so easily catch whoever the perpetrator was since the crime had occurred on intermittent days, even if it could be called a crime, since he had yet to establish a motive, but he needed to put a stop to whoever was using his boat, to nip it in the bud, as soon as possible.

Ah Bao felt more than a little anxious as he wound down along the steep path through stands of white pine, his calloused feet pounding the packed red earth, gripping the slippery rocks where the brooks and creeks crossed the path, coursing down the hill to feed the river. He wasn't sure what he would say or do if he encountered a culprit, but he thought he should begin to stoke the feelings of indignation he felt stirring within him. There was no way he could allow what was happening to continue.

As the trees began to thin and Ah Bao came out onto the narrow floodplain that lined the river's edge, still a good distance from the river, since the river's bank rose up slightly and was lined by tall grasses and sedges he could not see his boat where he normally beached it each day. He crouched down slightly and began to stealthily creep toward the beach behind the row of tall grasses. He didn't know what to expect but he prepared himself for the unexpected.

As he reached the line of grasses and sedges, slowly he stood up inch by inch to his full height so that he could see over the grass to the water's edge. Through the tops of the tall clumps of saw grass he could see his boat and knew in his attempt to catch the culprit he had been too late. His boat sat face up, hull against the sand. From the look of things, the hull still dripping water, he couldn't have missed the culprit by more than a few minutes. Looking up and down the beach he saw it was empty except for a familiar large gray mound about 50 meters down the beach.

He pushed aside the saw grass and walking up to the side of his boat he silently cursed his poor timing and vowed to himself that for his own piece of mind, and more importantly the security of his boat, without further delay he was going to catch whoever had been using his boat, and teach them a painful and unforgettable lesson.

CHAPTER TEN

Ah Bao decided he would need to take his investigative work to the next level. He quickly devised a plan where he would hide himself during the night in the tall grass on the crest of the river-bank, and lay in wait, and be certain to catch whoever had been using his boat. It might be an inconvenience for him, he would lose a little sleep because of it, but he began to worry that whoever was using his boat might put a hole in it, or wreck it, or even set it adrift, for it to float on down the river and be lost to him forever. Without a boat Ah Bao would soon go hungry and starve.

His plan was to return home from fishing, as usual, late in the afternoon, or early in the evening depending on how his fishing was going and his catch. He would go home, wash, and go to bed. He would allow himself to sleep well into the night, when he would rise, return to the riverside and mount his watch near his boat. He had decided it was imperative that he begin his vigil that very night.

Ah Bao looked back down the beach to where he had noticed a familiar large gray mound next to a couple of sizable rocks nestled, where they came together, between a V shaped row of grass. He draped his net over the side of the boat and strode quickly down toward the rocks. Then, just as he got within a few feet of the mound he heard a loud rumble, almost like a small clap of thunder, the gray mound shook ever so slightly, and a foul disgusting odor engulfed the immediate area of the beach and Ah Bao.

"Lao Shen," Ah Bao shouted, covering his nose and mouth, though his hand muffled his voice. Ah Bao, removing his hand from his nose and mouth, again shouted, "Lao Shen," and the gray blanket that covered the mound slowly slid back and revealed another rumbled mound beneath it. Slowly, one end of the mound rose up a little and transformed into a grizzled, dark brown face, hair tousled, myopic eyes squinting in the morning sunshine.

There was another small clap of thunder from beneath the blanket and another foul cloud drifted toward Ah Bao. "My heavens, Lao Shen, what have you been eating? You smell like an old, rotting dog carcass."

"What?" the old grizzled face asked, now twisted into a painful look of confusion, as he scratched the back of his head where his hair was matted in a filthy clump. "Why I haven't eaten a thing. At least not that I can remember, and if it was anything worth remembering... I'd remember it," with a brief pause to scratch the side of his head. "I drank something. When was that? Last night? Yes, last night. And that was only a little Xiaoxing wine, although it was very fine Xiaoxing wine." The old man gave Ah Bao a hopeful, though almost toothless smile, a yellow tooth in front, and two brown ones on one side of his mouth, all that remained of his teeth.

Ah Bao knew this to be a gross understatement. The old man was the town drunk, and during spring, summer, or autumn, late night, or early in the morning, if one were to go looking for the old man one could invariably find him sleeping here, or more accurately passed out in his usual haunt on the beach, where the sand had been washed away in a storm, and the beach provided a small overhand. Here one could fine him burrowed under his moth bitten, gray blanket.

"Well, fine then. But I want to ask you something, Lao Shen. And it's important. Maybe you were awakened this morning, by a voice, or a noise, and happened to see someone around my boat over there?" Ah Bao intentionally raised his voice a little as he spoke to the old man, since he was notoriously hard of hearing.

For a split second, Ah Bao considered the possibility that perhaps the old man might have taken the boat himself to drift down the river to find someplace to sleep undisturbed, but then immediately dismissed the idea, because of the wet hull, and knowing the old drunk didn't have the strength, or the probably the inclination to turn the heavy boat over, take it out on the water, and then return it to where it now sat. The old drunk didn't seem to have much of an inclination for anything, for that matter, besides to lift a bottle of spirits to his mouth.

"What boat?" The old man asked, confused, slowly looking around him as if seeing his surroundings for the very first time.

"My boat. That boat over there. You know where I always beach it down there." Ah Bao's voice had grown to a shout, and he pointed at his boat no more than fifty meters down the beach.

Lao Shen lay back down again, as if the whole affair had overwhelmed him, and was too much for him to even consider, and pulling his blanket back over his shoulder appeared to be going back to sleep. Then after only a moment he raised himself back up on one elbow, as if suddenly remembering something. "Boat, boat, boat," he said repeatedly, trying to jog his memory, looking down the beach through squinting, watery eyes, and with his free hand pulled at the few straggly hairs on his chin.

He slowly began to shake his head from side to side, not being able to make sense of what he was remembering. "Could it have been a little dog, or a fox, maybe? I think it was the other morning, over there, around your boat?" And he waved his shaky arm off toward the boat.

Then as if something had shocked him momentarily into some

inner realization, he said with certainty, "Yes. It was a dog. Or was it a fox, perhaps. Yes. I'm almost sure of it. Now leave me alone and let me sleep." And with that the old man slumped back down on the sand, rolled further under the overhang, and pulling the blanket back up over him, within a few moments was fast asleep, and snoring loudly.

Ah Bao realized he had wasted his time with Lao Shen, listening to the old man's drunken ramblings, and he turned, and strode back up the river bank to where his boat was beached. Laying his net in the bow of the boat, he inspected the boat quickly for any obvious damage. He then put his shoulder against the outside hull of the boat and pushed the boat out into the sandy shallows of the river. He picked up an oar and pushed off from the bottom propelling the boat slowly into the deeper emerald green water toward the center and the current of the river, and began to drift downstream.

Ah Bao fished that morning not fully concentrating on catching fish, distracted by his plans for that night. He saw a large carp roll in against a marshy area of the river, but once he had finally awoken from his reverie, and laid his net leading out from the marsh, the fish must have moved in another direction. When he pulled in his net it came up empty. This happened several times during the day when his thoughts so distracted him that it affected his fishing enough so that he kept missing the schools of fish that he knew were running in the river.

He told himself that there was something going on, he wasn't sure what, and he couldn't quite put his finger on it, that was just not quite right about what had been happening to his boat. He had never heard his father tell him about any thing similar occurring to his boat in earlier years, or had he heard any of the other villagers' talk about similar situations when they had gathered to talked about their catches or swap fishing stories. Why suddenly had this happened to him? He wondered if it might have had something to do with his parents death, or perhaps his recent interest in spiritual things.

Later he set his net further down the river in a stretch of the river that he was less familiar with, and in his distraction caught it on a large submerged log and torn a large hole in it. He cursed whoever was causing him to be so distracted, and vowed to take it out of their hide. Again and again he moved along the river laying his net, waiting a short while and then hauling it in, catching nothing. He had drifted down river most of the day, then put his shoulders to the oars and rowed the boat back up river from his normal landing place to a favorite fishing spot of his father's. Again he threw his net out, and then rested his boat patiently against the river bank waiting to see if any unsuspecting fish might swim into it. He hauled it in but it was empty.

Early that evening, tired and disappointed with his empty nets, and nothing to show for his hard work, wearily he rowed his boat back, beached it, trod up the path and returned home. Walking into the back courtyard he gave Wei Wei a half-hearted hello in answer to his twin barks, then washed himself from the bucket of water he drew from the well. Walking back into the cottage he lay down onto the cold kang and had no trouble falling asleep.

Later, when he opened his eyes and awoke he knew it was well past sundown. From the head of the kang in the northeast corner of the room he could see through the open back door the moon rising in the sky resting on a wispy strand of clouds. In the moonlight he also saw that Mei Mei had come with food and left without him knowing it. Walking over to the table and sitting down he lifted the lids of the dishes and saw she had brought him a plate of rice with a couple of small dried salted fish, a few pieces of pickled cabbage, and a small plate of peanuts. With his terrible luck at catching fish that day, even salted fish were a blessing, and Ah Bao silently thanked Mei Mei for her kindness.

After eating his meal, he took the peanuts which he had not eaten and poured them into his pocket. As darkness continued to fall he made his way down to the riverside. He found a comfortable mound of sandy earth behind the tall grass, about thirty meters from his boat. From his hiding place, parting the long tufts of grass, he could clearly see the rise where his boat lay next to the two clumps of saw grass, as well as being able to see the approaching landscape from both up and down the riverbank. He had saved the peanuts for a snack later during the night to help keep him awake. He sat down and began his watch.

During the first hour or two, as he waited, he had no trouble maintaining his concentration, focusing on what he could see of the riverbank, being as anxious as he was to unmask the culprit, see who it might be, and teach them a lesson. He slowly scanned to the left and right examining the surroundings, focusing his eyes in the moonlight, recognizing the familiar objects up and down the riverbank and along the shore. But, positioned as he was crouched in the grass, already tired from a day of fishing, the landscape became an unchanging pallet, and after the first two hours time refused to pass.

Poised from his hiding place behind the tall grass ready to spring down on the culprit, he soon became stiff from immobility, and his head became heavier and heavier with sleep. He would have liked to smoke but knew that the flame and smoke from the tobacco would surely have given him away from his hiding place, and besides he had not brought his tobacco, his pipe, or his papers, since he knew that it was out of the question. Instead he munched on the peanuts, one by one from his pocket, and tried to stay awake.

A cloud of sleep began to fill his head and though he fought it off objects in front of him began to swim back and forth. The throbbing that began in his lower legs and spread up his back he managed to chase away by massaging again and again the aching muscles in his stiff legs and back. By pinching himself on his arms and cheeks to force himself awake, he somehow managed to stay awake hidden in the grass. As the late night chill descended on the river and all the blood in his body settled in his organs he found himself thinking he was awake, then suddenly waking not sure how long he had been asleep. And unfortunately as the morning approached, and then shards of light slowly began to cut across the river as the sun began to rise in the sky, Ah Bao realized that the night's wait have proved anything but fruitful. When he had wanted it no one had come to try and take his boat.

Each successive night Ah Bao mounted his watch just as he had the first night. He brought with him in his pocket, a handful of dried sunflower seeds, or hawthorn berries from the wild haw bushes near his cottage to eat, and a pair of his fathers carved wooden dragon balls to roll in his hands, and to occupy his thoughts. And yet, each night it became harder for him to remain alert, squatting motionless in his hiding place, and even harder each successive night to remain awake, knowing that the previous nights' wait had revealed nothing.

CHAPTER ELEVEN

His hiding place was on a little hillock, a rise in the tall grass, behind a row of tall cattails and saw grass, so that, as he waited he was completely obscured from view. To ease the pain in his back and legs he experienced each night, he alternately began to sit cross legged, and then to sit with his legs sprawled out in front of him. Sometime he would allow his head to rest back on his hands against the rise of the hillock and look up at the countless stars above him. To pass the time he would recall the stories his father had told him about the various constellations.

It had been six days since he had begun his vigil, and on the seventh evening he made his way to his hiding place and sat down on the hillock. He rested his head back, the tall soft grass cushioning his head, and looked up at the stars and the three quarter moon that was rising in the sky. He took a few of the sweet dried hawthorn berries that he had carried with him in his pocket, and rolled them around in his mouth until they were soft. Then he began to chew on them slowly, and waited. He knew from the previous nights that his wait might be long and perhaps fruitless, but he would have to be patient. Looking at the moon and the constellation of the seven stars in the big dipper he hoped that would be auspicious since this was the seventh night he had waited. Then, looking up at the stars filling sky, from constellation to constellation, not knowing, he had closed his eyes for a moment, and was fast asleep.

He wasn't sure how long it had been that he had slept when he was startled awake by a scraping sound, and immediately recognized it as the sound of the hull of a boat scraping against the sandy bank of the river. Although he recognized it was a familiar sound, it was a moment or two before he cleared the sleep from his brain enough to open his eyes and see that the light of the approaching dawn was at hand. It startled him momentarily realizing he had slept the entire night. Through his half-closed sleepy eyes, his head still groggy, he parted the saw grass and cattails enough to look down from his rise on the hillock at the riverbank. And there his boat sat, once again dripping with water, the hull face down resting against the sandy riverbank.

It had finally happened again just as he had waited for. And yet there was no one within sight up or down the riverbank. How could that be? He had heard the sound of the boat scraping against the sand only moments before. In those few moments the sun had now peeked through the trees shining slivers of light down onto the river and he could clearly see the boat and all of its surroundings. But then what alarmed Ah Bao, and at the same time confused him, was that in the half light of the breaking dawn, the strands and wisps of fog rising off of the cold river, was that he was certain he could see, though it occurred in only a split second was what looked like a long gray brown fox, its ears tipped with black, it's chest and cheeks white, and tail tipped with white, as it jump from the boat onto the river bank, and then with a second bound disappear into the tall stand of grass beside him. He stood up quickly hoping to be able to look down into the boat and catch a glimpse of who was hiding there and must have carried the fox into the boat, but there was no one there.

Ah Bao, legs stiff and clumsy, stumbled from the hillock down to stand beside his boat. From beside the boat he could run his hand along the wet hull and could now see more clearly inside and around the boat, knowing that someone had to be hiding there. He looked for some unseen detail, but the boat was empty except for the oars which lay in the bottom of the boat, and the coil of new rope tied to the small anchor in its bow. And still he wondered how could someone have possibly taken the boat out onto the river, and then a moment ago returned it to the river bank without him seeing them. He slammed his fist against his open palm chiding himself for falling asleep, and knew he would probably have to stand watch again for who knew how many more nights before he would once again have an opportunity to catch the culprit.

CHAPTER TWELVE

Ah Bao dragged himself back up the hill to his cottage disappointed and confused. With a few small twigs and tinder he quickly made a small fire and heated some rice porridge. He gulped down a bowl of the hot congee, then hurriedly returned to his boat, and spent the day as usual fishing. That day with a little luck he caught several small fish. He returned home that afternoon after stopping at the Lus cottage, and finding no one at home left two of the larger fish hanging beside the door from from one of the hooks which Mrs. Lu usually hung chilis to dry in the fall. He had too many fish for his own meal but too few to spend the late afternoon trying to sell in the wet market. He was glad at least for a small opportunity to repay a little of Mei Mei and the Lus kindness.

Ah Bao then returned to his own cottage and took a long nap. He woke up shortly after sundown and ate the, then marched down to his hiding place by the river to begin his watch.
It was a bit easier for him to remain awake, now that he was certain that there was someone using his boat, and yet, he was possessed with a strange feeling that there was something peculiar, almost bizarre, about the circumstances surrounding his boat and whoever was using it. He couldn't put his finger on it, but it troubled him deeply.

But that night's watch, again no one came, and the boat sat where it lay throughout the night. Still Ah Bao didn't allow himself to become disheartened. Each successive night, after fishing during the day and taking a long nap in the evening, he continued to come to the hillock, and keep his vigil. What had been difficult at first to endure, had now taken on a routine, and he had been able to devise additional ways to keep himself from falling asleep besides pinching his arms and legs, and digging his knuckles into his cheeks.

Then on the seventh evening, after taking his evening nap, and waking to find a meal of rice, a fried fish, probably one of those he had left at the Lu's door earlier, some small bok choi, and some sauteed sweet potato leaves, that Mei Mei had once again brought over and left for him, he ate slowly and thoughtfully hopeful that tonight would be the night he would finally catch the culprit. Then as per his routine he marched down the hill and took up his post sitting as he had grown accustomed against the hillock. He rested his head back against the rise on his hands in a soft pillow of grass, and he looked up at the stars and the three quarter moon.

Hs belly filled and satisfied he thought about a time he and his father had gone fishing, shortly before his father's trip to Hong Kong and his death. They had drifted far down the river, and waiting to gather their nets, which they had laid across the leading edge of a marsh, his father had thrown a baited hook and line in close to the leeward end of the marsh. His father had hooked a huge black catfish which he had fought for the better part of an hour, it entangling itself in the reeds, his father fighting it free, then it entangling itself again. Each time it would turn its massive white belly up to the sun and roll over wrapping the line among the reeds. Although they both thought the fish was tiring and they would land it at any minute, it had finally broken the line and freed itself, and his father had lost the fish. In retrospect Ah Bao had wondered after his father's death if the loss of the fish had somehow been an omen of the old man's impending passing. As Ah Bao sat looking up at the moon and the stars he wondered what would happen if he would go back downstream on the river to where they had first encountered the fish, lurking in the tall reeds of that marsh. Might he too might be able to hook it? And what if this time be was able to land it? He could be sure it was the same fish because he was certain it must still bear the fishing hook buried deep in its upper lip. Would it help to appease his father's spirit and allow him to rest in peace? Not realizing it, he had closed his eyes, and after a few moments he was fast asleep dreaming about battling the catfish.

Perhaps it was providence, or a stroke of luck, or his father's own spirit that caused what happened next. Not long before dawn, a large spotted owl searching for mice in the tall grass, passed over near where Ah Bao lay sound asleep dreaming, and gave a loud screeching cry. The sound startled Ah Bao awake, and gasping, almost choking on his own tongue, he jerked awake. He bolted up into a sitting position so hard, he almost somersaulted himself forward through the grass to roll down the riverbank. Luckily he steadied and caught himself with his hands in front of him, and after a moment looked hard through his sleepy, half closed eyes down toward the riverbank. The boat was gone. Suddenly he knew that this night his luck had changed. For a moment he thought with a fright that perhaps this time someone had taken the boat and would not return, and then taking a deep breath he calmed himself and forced himself to believe that tonight would take the same course as other earlier nights and the culprit would return, this time to be caught red-handed.

He rubbed his eyes hard and slapped his cheeks, trying to quickly bring himself fully awake. He wished he could walk down to the riverside and splash cold water on his face but knew he could not jeopardize his hiding place. After a long hour's wait the false dawn began to show the outlines and then the shapes of objects along the river's edge. Like a ghost appearing through the mist of the morning fog, Ah Bao could see the shape of a boat moving across the river, and immediately recognized it as his own. Slowly he began to crawl along the crest of the riverbank until he was level with the low spot on the bank where he was almost certain the boat would be brought onto the bank and beached.

Each moment the light was growing more strongly, things around him were taking shape, and he knew dawn was only moments away, which would make it easier to expose the identity of the perpetrator. As he raised his head higher to give himself a better view of the low place between where the twin hillocks lay, and the boat would normally be brought ashore, through the mist he could hear the hull of his boat beginning to scrape against the sand of the shallow river bottom of the shore, and then the louder scrap as it rose up, and then thudded against the bank. At the same time, through the rising mist he could see the shape of someone crouching low in the bow of the boat, as if preparing to jump ashore.

Ah Bao planned the direction of his attack, and held his breath still hidden by the tall grass. He knew he must wait for the person to step onto the bank, and begin to pull the boat up toward its resting place, and as they turned their back to him he could grab them, and subdue them, catching them off guard.

Then, just as he had planned, as the person jumped ashore, turning his back toward him, Ah Bao rose up out of the grass. Bounding down the riverbank and pounced on the bandit. Gripping the person's arms from behind he trapped them tightly against the culprit's chest.

A startled, ear piercing scream by the culprit struck Ah Bao's ears, and turning, struck him as well, hard on the side of the head, with an elbow, at exactly the place where he had been struck years before by the falling flowerpot. Ah Bao stumbled to the ground, momentarily losing consciousness. When he awoke, Ah Bao realized hastily, he had released his grip from the thief.

Ah Bao had prepared himself for resistance, a fight, words of false protest, and though the startled scream had surprised him, and although it was the blow to his head that made him fall down, there was something else, the moment before, that had made him release his grip. Ah Bao had been shocked, amazed, at how strangely soft , though supple, and unresisting the culprit's body felt under his arms, and it had so surprised him that he had immediately released his grip, and jumped back.

CHAPTER THIRTEEN

In that instant, when the dark figure spun toward him, in the half predawn light Ah Bao realized his culprit was a young woman. Looking up at her, Ah Bao wasn't sure who had been more surprised; he or the young woman, though he realized his mouth had fallen open, and stayed open while he lay on the ground, in front of her, dumb struck, unable to speak.

Though the young woman's hair falling across her back was untied, and unbraided, slightly disheveled, the skin of her cheeks was a creamy alabaster white, her features so fine it was as if they had been drawn on her skin with the finest of brushes. At that moment the only thought that filled Ah Bao's mind as he looked up at her was that this woman seemed to him the loveliest person he had ever seen. He was certain she was not from either his village, or the city. In fact, she was unlike any Henan women he had ever seen.

Finally, when he regained what he thought was his self composure, though as he stared up at the lovely creature in front of him, he felt his heart begin to bound in his chest like a drum, and his mouth dry as paper. He wanted to speak but couldn't. Then after some difficulty, wetting his mouth enough to croak a few words, he demanded of her, in as accusing a tone as he could muster, "What gave you the right to take my boat?"

He reached out to grab her arm again, to prevent her from trying to escape, but then thinking better of it, rubbed the place on the side of his head where she had hit him instead. The young woman herself seemed unable to speak. Her eyes were wide with fear, the look of a trapped fawn in the snare of the hunter. She wrung her hands again, and again, and after some time seeming to give her enough courage, she eventually was able to answer. Her voice was soft and barely audible, yet filled with a vulnerable ache as if at that moment she might break into sobbing tears. Ah Bao looking at her shoulders and could see she was trembling. "Sir," she said, then stopped, her eyes welling with tears. "Please forgive me, won't you, but I really haven't meant to steal your boat, only to borrow it."

"Well, if that's the case I don't see there's much of a difference," Ah Bao, said, now a little more in control of his senses, trying to sound indignant. "All right, then. Why have you borrowed my boat, so presumptuously, not even bothering to ask my permission? That is, presuming of course, for some absurd reason I might have allowed you to use it."
"Oh, Sir, you don't understand. My time is so short," she said, pausing, as if trying to find just the right words, and watching the horizon over Ah Bao's shoulder as it began to lighten. As her eyes shifted from his eyes to the horizon, and back again, Ah Bao sensed she might try to escape, and he stepped in her way to block her retreat down the riverbank. "You don't understand how difficult my story is to tell, and I'm afraid perhaps you'll find it even harder to believe. I've used your boat simply to look for my family who I've lost," she said, searching his eyes for forgiveness.

Quickly, as if pursued by some inner demon, during the next few minutes as the light of dawn was beginning to break, the lovely young woman tried to explain her circumstances, her words coming rapidly, almost breathlessly from her pale lips, her eyes darting furtively toward the lightening horizon.

"I am called Aymer, she told Ah Bao. "My family is from a a ways West of here in the province of Xinjiang, and my ancestors have lived near the city of Urumqi for centuries. The head of our family has always been a tribal chief; a chief among chiefs. Although years ago our family chief was considered a prince we no longer use that title.

"A month ago we, my father, my mother, and my brother and I had come here with a caravan of pack animals, camels and horses, laden with dates and melons to sell. When we reached a place up river from here my father decided it would be more expeditious if we came the rest of the journey by water. We moved our cargo onto a large boat and were traveling on the river together, but our cargo was to heavy even for the large boat." At this Aymer stopped for a moment as if trying to compose herself before continuing.

Tragically, she said, there had been an accident. It had occurred almost a month before, as they were coming down the river just above where they stood, on a windy afternoon, the river rough, the choppy water coming over the sides. In the rough water the boat had swamped under the heavy load and capsized, and her entire family had been swept into the river. Having never lived near water, trying to help each other, her father trying to save her young brother, his mother and brother holding each other, they had drowned together. She told Ah Bao that she too had been swept into the treacherous currents, though separated from them by a distance, and a powerful undertow had drawn her down beneath the swirling eddies. She had lost total consciousness, and the next thing she knew she was floating in the ebb tide along the shoals, her eyes closed, her lips barely resting above the surface of the water, her head pounding. Through the pounding the sound of a thundering voice seemed to be beating against her ears. She realized she must be confronting some omniscient spirit of some kind that had unexplained powers over the river, and the voice spoke to her.

The voice of the spirit beating in her ears had told her that she must accept that her family had perished. She hadn't wanted to believe the voice that said her parents and her small brother were lost to her, but the spirit's deafening sounds, repeating those words over and over had convinced her. As she had pulled herself onto the shore of the river she begged the spirit that confronted her, to give her the strength to allow her to try and search for them.

The spirit had agreed to her pleas, but it insisted that she must first rest, and regain her strength. The voice told her she would be allowed to search for the bodies of her family for the period of one lunar month. Furthermore, she would only search for them for one night at each quarter of the new moon, as it waxed, and the moon became full.

This she had done, she told Ah Bao, for three phases of the moon, the spirit of the river had allowed her to search for her family, but she had been unable to find them. She would have one final opportunity; the last chance she would be given was a week from that night, on the night it would wax to a full moon. If she was unable to find and recover their bodies, and give them a proper burial, their souls would forever float through the afterlife, troubled spirits, unable to find a resting place.

"I hope you can understand these unbearable feelings I have, and be able to forgive me," she said finally, her hands clasped together beseeching Ah Bao for his help. "And know that I have had no other choice but to borrow your boat."

Aymer stood in front of him, searching Ah Bao's eyes for some sign of compassion, her own filling with tears, and a look of heartbreaking sorrow, and she said in almost a whisper, "Could you possibly, could you find it in your heart to help me try and recover the bodies of my parents, and my young brother? That way, I wouldn't be forced to asked to borrow your boat. If you could, I would forever be in your debt. And I will tell you, if it will make a difference in your decision, that my father had a large purse of gold and silver coins with him when he was washed over the side of the boat."

Looking in her eyes Ah Bao realized one of the things that made Aymer's eyes so beautiful was that although they weren't as full as Henan girls, or not as thin as Han women, it was that Aymer's eyes turned up only slightly below her eyebrows pointed toward her hairline, and made her look a little like a fox.

Standing beside Aymer, Ah Bao suddenly felt a tiredness, an overpowering dizziness, as the rays of the dawn light broke in front of him, across the river above the eastern ridge, blinding him for a moment, and Ah Bao closed his eyes. At that moment, before he could answer her questions, Aymer appeared to turn away from him for a split second, almost to shrink, as if she was overcome with shame, and in that same moment her clothes seemed to fall from her arms, and body, to fall away like a curtain falling from a window, a curtain releasing her spirit, and Aymer seeming to vanish with the dawn light.

Ah Bao was so startled by Aymer's sudden disappearance, he rubbed his eyes thinking perhaps he must still be asleep, and looked quickly around him, and up and down the riverbank to see if perhaps the young woman had run away somewhere to escape. She was nowhere to be seen. Then a second later, a rustling in the pile of clothes at Ah Bao's feet, the light still dim below the riverbank, revealed a gray fox slipping from beneath them.

CHAPTER FOURTEEN

What had just happened? Ah Bao felt like he was in shock, wondering could it even have happened? Had the young woman through some slight of hand or body slipped from her robes and disappeared into the tall grasses without him seeing her? Was it some coincidence that this gray fox had perhaps slipped past him from beside the boat underneath the clothes, looking for something, and then startled run off toward the riverbank, and the grass, as well? Ah Bao searched his brain for some way to account for the frightening possibilities of what had just occurred, and was at a loss for even some wildly plausible explanation.

Was this the same gray fox that he had thought he had seen darting away from his boat the week before? Now he wasn't even sure that day he had, in fact, seen a fox. But then old Lao Shen had mentioned a dog, or a fox, too. Looking down the riverbank Ah Bao saw the fox pause, gaze back at his shocked face, then turn back and run from where it stood on the riverbank, bounding into the tall grass.

Ah Bao leaned against his boat, his hand resting on the wet keel, suddenly feeling very tired, his knees trembling, knocking against each other, almost unable to support him. He wondered if living alone for the past year, except for the occasional visit from Mei Mei quacking at him, had caused him to imagine what had just happened? Or perhaps he was still asleep. He slapped his face sharply, trying to startle himself from a dream, but this only had the effect of leaving him with a stinging pain in his cheek, and he had to accept, in fact, he was, indeed, wide awake, which frightened him even more. His knees slowly gave way buckling under him, and he slid down the side of his boat slumping to the ground, his breath coming in short gasps.

Why had this happened to him? What had he done to deserve this? Was it some offense that he had made to his parents spirits in the past weeks that had caused them to bring this woman-fox apparition to torment him and take his boat? Should he have been performing the bai bai in the evening as well as in the morning to show his filial respect? The young woman was indeed beautiful, he had to admit that, but why had she chosen him and his boat? There were other fishermen with other boats that she might have chosen as easily. Still, her lovely face and beseeching words had an intense effect on Ah Bao, and he was convinced that fate had somehow brought her lovely presence to him. Was there some tie between the lose of his own parents and the lose of her family? Perhaps it was a trial of some kind, a test of his own character and his love for his parents.

But, then again, what if this young woman named Aymer had been sent by some evil force against him? He had to believe, or at least consider, that she was easily transforming herself back and forth between a fox and the gorgeous young woman that had spoken to him and had repeatedly taken his boat. Perhaps it had something to do with the spirits of the river. Perhaps he had done something to offend the powers over the river and they were trying to entice him, to draw him unsuspecting to his own death, further down the river on the treacherous stretch of shoals beyond the marshes. He must be very careful, he told himself. Even if he decided to help her, he could be dangerously tricked by some unknown forces into losing his boat, or even his own life.

CHAPTER FIFTEEN

Sitting against his boat, calming himself, Ah Bao tried to rid his mind of all emotion and think clearly about what had happened. From what Aymer had told him, he calculated, if for some reason he decided that he might help her, he would wait for the moon to continue to wax another quarter, or a period of seven days, just as he had waited unaware of this enforced delay between the previous encounters. He hoped too that this meant she would not try to take his boat again before then and he might not be distracted by this interference and disruption in his daily routine. Then, on the night of the full moon, he surmised that he might be allowed to discover what was the girl's true mission. He had to conclude that whether he decided to help her or not that this could have an indelible affect on what the future held in store for him.

Thinking about her now, and the beseeching way in which she had looked at him and spoken to him, he couldn't distract himself from how astonishingly beautiful she was. He told himself that perhaps if he helped her this would also please his parents spirits and allow them some peace in the afterlife. He told himself he didn't even want to consider the gold that she had mentioned because he couldn't be sure of its truth, and if he did assist her he would have to do it altruistically for there to be any possibility of it providing any succor for his parents spirits. But what rattled him more than a little was he realized he was already being drawn to her, becoming captivated by her words, and her beauty. Ah Bao told himself that although he wanted to help Aymer because of her expression of filial piety, and which could help to continue to reinforce his own, he couldn't let his altruism blind him, and he must be cautious against any deception from whatever forces were weaving the unexplainable circumstances that might lead to harm him.

Ah Bao pulled himself up from where he was sitting beside the boat and struggled back up the hill to his cottage. As he was crossing the road to enter his courtyard he could see Mei Rong just as she was about to turn the bend in the road as it wound in toward the village. She must have been watch through the pine trees as he mounted the hill because she had stopped too and looked back at him on the road. She waved, and he thought he could see her smile, then turned and disappeared around the bend in the road.

Seeing Mei Mei at that moment, and thinking about her acts of kindness toward him interrupted the turmoil and indecision he was feeling from that morning. Ah Bao, for the briefest moment, allowed himself to rejoice at Mei Mei's pure and unmitigated expression of goodness toward him. He realized she was no beauty, as Aymer was, and although he wanted to believe in her heart Aymer was a good person, at the same time there had never been any alternation of any kind in Mei Mei's being, or her spirit, and he truly believed that what she did, independent of her mother's influence, had no other motivation than that she cared for him, and only wished for his affection, and he naively hoped she would always care for him no matter what else might transpire in the world around them.

But what Ah Bao wished for more than anything at that moment, as he entered his courtyard and sat down to rest on the bench under the stone pine was guidance either in the form of some sign that might present itself to him and explain things, or in the way of advice from someone much wiser than himself. If only his father was still alive he would certainly know what to do. His understanding of the river, and the power the spirits had over the river, and his understanding of life in general was much greater than his own, and Ah Bao wondered if what had transpired to him, if the older man were still alive would have even taken place. Ah Bao was certain of one thing; that the young woman's beauty would have little sway over his father, and if he were given the choice of whether or not to help her, although he might agree, Aymer's charms would have little effect on the older man. Or would they? And what was the tie between Aymer and the gray fox?

Ah Bao thought about the old monk from the temple and what advice he might be able to give him. He too had a greater understanding of nature and the world around him than Ah Bao possessed. Would he be able to explain the strange happening that had taken place at the riverside? Whether or not he could explain those things he couldn't be called on at that moment to help Ah Bao. And Ah Bao was so vexed by what had happened that morning that he couldn't bring himself to go back down to the river and go out fishing. His only recourse, what he hoped would be his immediate salvation was to try to find some answer in the book which the monk had lent him.

Going into the cottage he picked up the small leather bound volume and brought it back out into the sun to sit and try to find some answer, some meaning which would elucidate what had just happened. He knew from struggling with the readings before that although the text, the words were simply written, the depth and truth which they held within them were multifold. Opening to the first passage he began to read.

He knew, after having repeated read the first lines of the first passage, the words from the lines almost by memory, if not their meaning. "What can be told of the Tao is not the eternal Tao, and what can be named is not the eternal name. The nameless is the beginning of heaven and earth, and the named is the mother of the ten thousand things." The lines were so simple yet so deep.

Then the next two lines that followed made him pause and stop reading and think more deeply still. "Ever desireless, one can see the mystery. Ever desiring, one can see the manifestations. These two spring from the same source but differ in name; this appears as darkness. Darkness within darkness. The gate to all mystery."

He realized that the moment he had laid eyes on her he had immediately desired the beautiful Aymer.   And yet what he also wanted was to be able to understand the manifestations of what had occurred, at least what he thought he saw occur at the riverside. But what he believed the book was saying was that he would need to be desireless to be able to see what the dark forces were that combined to obscure his understanding and mystify him?

He read on through the next passage.   "All can see beauty as beauty because there is ugliness, all can know good because there is evil. Having and not having arise together, difficult and easy complement each other, high and low rest upon each other, long and short contrast each other, front and back follow one another. The wise man proceeds by doing nothing, working yet not taking credit. Work is done then forgotten."

Ah Bao tried to find a clue in this passage though his head was beginning to swim with all the words. Was it telling him that he should try and ignore Aymer's beauty and simply help her because he could and not worry about the fact that he was helping her? Then he could forget about it and things would take care of themselves? He tried to assure himself that perhaps he was making too much of what had happened with the gray fox that morning. Somehow this didn't seem to fully explain it, although he told himself he would try to read the passages again and focus on the meaning and perhaps this would reassure him.

But first he needed to give his head a rest from all the words and thoughts and go fishing and try to catch some fish. He told himself that this the book was also telling him; that he should do his work of fishing and let the other things for the time being take care of themselves. He closed the book, and after taking it back into the cottage and putting it back on the shelf where he kept it, he came back out slung his net over his shoulder and went down to the river to fish. Although the book was giving him a great deal to think about, he felt his father's spirit was telling him to get to work.

CHAPTER SIXTEEN

As the days of the next week began to pass Ah Bao tried to stay busy with fishing, pushing himself to go further down the river than usual, almost to the marshes, laying his net often, and retrieving it, giving the fish enough time to become trapped in the net, but hopefully not allowing his mind time to attach itself to thoughts that were unrelated to fishing. His arms, back, and legs burned with the effort of his work and he was rewarded each day with large catches of fish trapped in his net. And yet, when he was awake he found it impossible to keep his mind on what he was doing. While he was fishing, water streaming off of the glistening side of a struggling fish would remind Ah Bao of Aymer's lovely flowing hair, or the graceful shape of her body beneath her robes. The depths of a dark clear pool reminded him of her lovely sable colored eyes. And what was hardest for him to forget was the soft resilience of her body beneath his hands. Then at night, when he slept, in the boundless imagination of his dreams, he encountered Aymer waiting for him. Now, though, unlike her face at the riverside sad and beseeching him, in his dreams she was smiling and vibrant, her arms inviting. And during the release of his dreams he felt all the solitude he had experienced since his parents' death melting away, and willingly he allowed his heart and body to be drawn toward her apparition.

But as the week continued to pass, his thoughts invariably return to the moment a the riverside when Aymer had been transformed into something else. Now, as the days passed, he wasn't sure at that moment when the dawning light broke above the mountains if she in fact had transformed into a fox, or some half fox half woman spirit. He tried to consider the manifestations that were possible. He wondered if she, the fox, or fox-woman, could change back into Aymer at any moment. He had begun to think of her that way more and more, envisioning her as a fox, and in the way in which she had appeared to be transformed into an animal and then envisioning her changing back into a woman. He fixed on the idea if he thought of her in this way he was less likely to be drawn in and capitavated by her lovely female charms when they would meet again. And Ah Bao had decided that they must meet again.

The fifth and sixth days and nights were frustrating slow in passing. During the days he was distracted, unable to concentrate on his fishing. At night he tossed and turned, his sleep fitful and troubled by wild unimaginable dreams that made no sense to him at all. Then, at last, the seventh day arrived. The day had finally arrived when he and the lovely Aymer would meet again, and he felt on the verge of exhaustion.

He tried to fish that day setting his nets repeatedly and catching almost nothing. His head felt like a large rock sitting atop his shoulders and he could barely think so he had decided to try return home early and get some rest before having to rise along with the full moon that night. Reaching the courtyard to the cottage he passed through the small courtyard and as he was about to enter the cottage from the corner of his eye he realized the old monk from the nearby Jinhua Temple who had lent him the book of scriptures was sitting under the stone pine tree. The monk had been seated unmoving, perhaps meditating as he waited on the bench. When Ah Bao saw him and turned toward him he saw that the old monk was smiling.

"Ah, my young friend, it has been a long time. How have you been? Have you been reading those scriptures I gave you?" The old monk chuckled as if he already knew the answer.

"Old brother, you've finally come. Welcome to my home," Ah Bao answered sincerely happy to see the old monk and have someone knowledgeable to talk to and perhaps answer his doubts about the strange and disturbing things that had taken place during the past weeks. " Yes, yes, I've been reading. Not as much as I should perhaps, but the book seems to be saying so much to me." Ah Bao knew that inevitably when he would pick up the book of scriptures, and read the short passages, it would cause him to become lost in thought, and then not read on.

"Well, then tell me how have you been? Have you been fishing?"

"Yes, old brother, I've been fishing. But please excuse my discourteousness. I don't want to be impolite and change the subject, but we need to talk about other things. Strange things that have happened." Ah Bao was so excited to see the monk and anxious about what had happened at the river that he wanted to speak about it immediately. "Let me not be a rude host though. First let me get you something to drink," Ah Bao said rushing into the house to retrieve the teapot and a couple of empty cups.

As Ah Bao came back out and sat down next to the old monk, and began to pour each of them a cup of cold tea the events of the preceding week flooded his brain. Where should he begin. Here was someone he could confide in, and might be able to give him advice, and yet he felt giddy not knowing where to begin. How would anyone, even this monk who had an understanding of nature and the world around him, believe such a wild and outrageous story?

"Let me ask you something, old brother," Ah Bao said, looking hard into the eyes of the old monk, hoping he would take him seriously and not think him insane. Then after a long pause Ah Bao continued, "I know you will think it is impossible to believe, but what would you say if I told you I thought a woman, a woman who can change herself into a fox has been using my boat and taking it out on to the river? I know, I know. It's really too strange to believe, but I tell you this because, I saw it with my own eyes, touched her with my hand, and I fear for the worse. I'm afraid my boat is going to be damaged." As Ah Bao mentioned touching Aymer, he felt himself blush briefly, and hoped his embarrassment didn't show.

"Oh, yes, young friend, you're right. This is indeed strange and mysterious." The old monk agreed nodding slowly, and began to gently stroke his long wispy beard. And yet, the tone of his voice didn't sound the least bit amazed. "Let me see if I can put it into perspective for us to be able to understand." The old monk paused for a long moment and slowly took a sip of his tea. He stroked his beard a couple more times then he closed his eyes for a long while as if lost in thought. Ah Bao thought the old monk might have fallen asleep as he sat anxiously waiting for an answer.

Then the monk began to speak again. "Well, now, young brother. What would you say if I told you that rather than a fox that a rock had damaged your boat. A cold lifeless, inanimate object such as a rock damaging your boat? Would that not seem just as implausible? And yet, with the proper circumstances I'll wager you can see how that might happen, am I correct?

"Boats are damaged all the time by rocks in the rivers, and rocks on the shore. I'm sure you can tell me of numerous times that this has happened to boats you know of. Now let's replace a cold inanimate physical object like a rock, with a living, breathing, thinking creature such as a fox, and with the proper circumstances I think we should be able to see how this too might happen. Why should it be so hard to imagine that a fox could damage a boat when one understands all the circumstances involved, right?" The old monk was smiling again, this time with a slightly quizzical look on his face, as if he was perplexed that Ah Bao had not seen this obvious answer to his own question.

But at that moment Ah Bao would happily have accepted that rational explanation of the fox that the monk had provided if the monk could only explain away the other outrageous details of the circumstances which had filled his life during recent weeks. Would the old monk be able to make sense out of them, as well. How would the monk be able to explain away the beautiful young woman, Aymer, and how she had changed into the fox? Would he be able to provide a rational explanation for that too?

As if reading his thoughts the monk stroked his beard again twisting the long wispy hairs around his index finger, then stopped with a chuckle. "Again, my young friend, is it so hard for you to accept that a young woman, whether beautiful or ugly for that matter, might have taken your boat out on the river to use for some reason? Do with know the reason?" At this, as Ah Bao began to speak, to volunteer an answer, the old monk held up his hand to cut him off. "Yes, you'll accept that part of the scenario as plausible also, correct?"

"What seems to be troubling you is how could a young woman turned herself into a fox, or perhaps how a fox turned itself into a woman, right?" The old monk didn't wait for an answer but continued on. "Don't allow the woman's beauty, or the mystery that you have experienced blind you to what has happened. Every winter something as simple as melting ice becoming water occurs, and yet what actually causes that transformation from solid ice to liquid water? The Spring is warm, the ice melts and turns to water, but if we are unable to easily explain what causes it than it is a mystery and hard for us to accept.

"How does the caterpillar make the metamorphosis into a butterfly? It is something we don't completely understand yet it is something in nature we accept without really questioning it. Should we do the same for this metamorphosis between this fox and this woman?"

"Well, I guess so," Ah Bao said confident that the old monk was guiding him to a logical conclusion, though he was not really convinced that he could accept it.

"Ah, young friend this is the doorway to mystery. This is one of the ten thousand things, though it is not one we see very often. Perhaps we shouldn't be so quick to accept it at face value until we see what the butterfly, so to speak, will do. Does this make sense to you?"

"I think so," Ah Bao answer, and although a little more confident with the monk's explanation, still not completely sure what he should prepare himself to expect that night, and deduced from the monk that he should rightly be feeling uncertain, when he went down to the river to meet Aymer.

"Keep the book, my young friend, and continue to read.   Although fear is one of the five emotions, a healthy response to manifestations, you mustn't let it overpower your understanding. As the scriptures ask you, 'Must you fear what others fear? This is nonsense. It is all right to be confused. Be like a newborn babe before it learns to smile. The great mother will nourish you.' I will return again. This time I will return much sooner. Perhaps tomorrow. Now I must go. 'Rest and empty yourself of everything. Let the mind rest at peace.' " At this, the old monk patted Ah Bao on his shoulder, drained his teacup, rose and disappeared out of the courtyard gate.

CHAPTER SEVENTEEN

Ah Bao went into the cottage to eat something before he lay down to rest but found that he had no appetite. It was still light out but he lay down on the kang and closed his eyes. Although thoughts of the possible outcomes of what might take place that evening swam dizzily in his head, he trying to empty himself and allow his mind to rest at peace, as the monk had suggested. Slowly he felt his breathing relax and after a few moments he fell soundly asleep.

Awaking later in the dark, Ah Bao immediately knew he had over-slept, and panic stricken he leaped up from his bed. He tried to get control of himself as he gathered his nets in one arm and left the cottage. Half running, half walking, he made his way as quickly as he could down to the riverside. His head still felt clouded with sleep, and his legs felt like he was floating on air as he hurried down toward the river. As he reached the bottom of the hill he was out of breath, and stopped for a moment to catch his breath.

Then continuing on down to the side of the river he parted the tall saw grasses and came out onto the riverbank to where he had left his boat. The boat appeared to have been unmoved. He scanned the riverbank but neither Aymer nor any sign of the gray fox was anywhere in sight. In the moonlight he could see that the hull of the boat was dry but ran his hand along the side for reassurance. He leaned up against the boat, resting against the side of it trying to fully catch his breath. Then, hearing a noise in the grass behind him, he turned and saw Aymer emerge from the exact place where he had stood his nightly vigil on those nights before they had met. As she approached him he looked directly into her eyes which reflected the luminous moon from above. Aymer lowered her gaze, and though they didn't speak, she half bowed to him repeatedly, as if at finding that he had agreed to help her, she wished to show some small way her gratitude.

Together they heaved against the hull of the boat and turned it over. As they pushed the boat bow first into the water, Ah Bao wondered how Aymer had been strong enough to accomplish this by herself.   Then Aymer jumped in and sat down in the bow of the boat, and as the boat cleared the sandy bottom Ah Bao jumped in and took the seat at the oars in the middle of the boat. As the current pulled the boat into the river, Aymer leaned forward as if searching the dark waters for some sign, then raised her hand and pointed down river. As they began to float down river Ah Bao felt he was somehow able to guess Aymer's thoughts, with only an oc-casional motion with her hand to move further this way or that way down the river, and he guided the boat down the river hug-ging close to the riverbank.

The moon was bright on the water, Ah Bao easily maneuvering the boat down the river, and he was confident that they wold be able to locate the area where Aymer wished to arrive at, though what they would find there he wasn't sure of yet. Then, after some time, they reach a certain point on the river, just past a long half submerged pine log that jutted out into the water from below a high sandstone bluff, which Ah Bao knew well, and Aymer raised her hand signaling for Ah Bao to slow the boat. He dug his oars into the current, turning the boat sideways, and then upriver, and threw out the small anchor. After a few moments, the boat slowed its momentum, its bow facing upriver, and held its place in the water. Aymer slowly scanned the chop of the dark waves, then glanced back at Ah Bao, and motioned to the net.

Taking one end of his net as he would usually do when he was fishing, he threw the weighted end of it over the side. Easing up on the anchor, he allowed his boat to slowly float down the river as he fed out the length of the net. As if instinctively knowing what to do, as Ah Bao had moved forward in the boat to feed out the net Aymer had taken his place at the oars in the middle of the boat, and pulling against them had guided the boat toward the opposite bank of the river. Once Ah Bao had payed out the net to its other end, and still holding the end of the net, Aymer had almost reached the far bank of the river. Then as Aymer turned the boat gradually back up river, Ah Bao began to gather in the net seining it in like a purse.

As Ah Bao gathered in the net he thought to himself how competent Aymer was at the oars of the boat, for a woman who had never worked fishing. He wished he could simply marvel at her abilities, though there was something about her skill that frightened him a little and wondered if there was something else behind it. He tried to brush it off remembering what the monk had told him about unjust fear and to concentrate on the task at hand.

Together they laid the net numerous times in the fast moving current, each time floating down the river a short distance further from the sandstone bluff than the previous try, and each time all that was recovered were scraps of wood and trash. Arm over arm Ah Bao gathered in the net, and having only allowed the net to set for a short while, there were no fish, though each time there were small waterlogged pieces of flotsam, some wood, shards of an old bowl, a rusted utensil, or a broken toy, lodged in the webbing of the net. Each of these he would quickly extract from the net throwing it over his shoulder back into the water, and continued gathering in the net and straightening the dripping lines.

As the night wore on Ah Bao began to see the futility in their efforts. He felt that if he could help Aymer recover what she could of her families remains than that was the right thing to do, but their efforts appeared to be useless. Perhaps it had been too long since their drowning and their remains had been washed on down the river or consumed by the creatures of the river.

Then, during one of the countless times he retrieved the dripping net from the river, he saw what appeared to be a long bleached piece of wood lodged in the webbing. The boat had passed beneath a stand of trees that was partially blocking the moonlight and though Ah Bao couldn't see clearly he grabbed a hold of what appeared to be more woody detritus to extract it from the webbing of the net and throw it back into the water. Touching it, the shock of the feel of cold clammy flesh made him realize it was not wood at all but a human arm. As the boat shifted slightly and the moon shone more clearly down on him, he could see that the arm reached out from the water, a half opened hand at the end of it. Taking a hold of the wrist in his own hand, he turned and looked back at Aymer to tell her he had recovered something. Just as he did the arm rotated in his grasp, the hand closing in a vise-like grip grabbing on to his own forearm.

The hair on the back of Ah Bao's neck stood up as straight as on the back of a startled cat. Ah Bao stared transfixed into the net, and as he pulled back from the force of the hand a body attached to the hand rose and partially emerged from the water. The head of the body cleared the water, a ghoulish expression on its face, its eyes rolled back in its head, a deathly grin stretching across its face, and as the rest of its body pushed, rolling against the side of the boat, it began to pull Ah Bao down into the river. The vise-like grip of the hand refused to release Ah Bao, an overwhelming panic gripped his heart. Although Ah Bao wanted to yell, to scream out, no sound would escape his lips.

Suddenly, jerking repeatedly in a spasm of terror he found himself awake, bolt upright in his bed, trembling, covered with sweat. Ah Bao realized in astonishment that it had only been a dream. He looked up toward the window, and from the rapidly approaching evening twilight realized that the sun had already set and he had slept only for perhaps an hour or so, and yet the dream had seemed so real.

Ah Bao sat on the kang reconsidering whether he was wise in going to the river and helping Aymer. He tried to convince himself that it was in his own best interests to help her because he knew if he didn't that she would try to take his boat out without him and that could easily end in tradgedy. And yet his dream had left him so shaken that he wasn't sure he could bring himself to get up and go down to the river. He wished he could just lie back down and dream away all that had happened but he knew that wasn't possible.

He tried to bolster his courage and told himself it was already getting dark, and if he was going to help Aymer he must go to the riverside immediately. And yet the nightmare had completely drained him of the whatever courage he had previously possessed. It took all of his strength for Ah Bao to raise himself out of his bed, and force his feet over the side of the kang and to get up. He kept reminding himself of what the old monk had said to him about not fearing what others feared, and that mother nature would nourish him, but the few hours that had passed since seeing the monk was enough time to make him reconsider.
Looking across the room at the photos of his parents sitting against the wall reminded Ah Bao of the reasons that Aymer was so desperate in her hunt for her own parents remains, and Ah Bao told himself that placed in her position he too might resort to similarly dire measures. He decided that he must do it, steel his heart against emotion, and follow the steps in his dream back down the hill to the river.

CHAPTER EIGHTEEN

This time when he reached the bottom of the hill he didn't experience the breathlessness of his dream which helped to settle his nerves. As he approached the crest of the bank of the riverside, once again he could see that the young woman was nowhere in sight. Then, as if his dream was replaying itself before him, Aymer stepped from the tall grass where he had stood watch each night. This time, though, without hestation she spoke to him. "I was doubtful you would come. But please, Sir, now that you are here know that I will be forever grateful for your helping me. And again, let me remind you that if we recover my father's gold it is all yours to keep."

"I understand what you're saying," he said, "but I, too, recently lost my parents, and the reason I'm helping you has nothing to do with any monetary gain." He wanted to be sure she understood that he had no ulterior motives for helping her. "And please, my name is Chang Ah Bao," he added. "Call me Ah Bao. If I am going to help you, let's not be on such formal terms."

Now that he was in her presence again, he felt inextricably drawn to her both because of her beauty and something undefinable in the young woman's self assured manner that put him at ease, though once out on the water he knew he would need to remain vigilant. That, and the fact that he still had a nauseating feeling of dread in the pit of his stomach for the night's work ahead on the river. He couldn't completely shake off the feelings from his earlier nightmare.

Together they heaved against the hull of the boat and turned the boat over. As the boat rolled over onto its hull, Aymer said, "I'm afraid we must hurry, now. The time that I have remaining to try and find my family, to recover their bodies, is short. That is if I am fortunate enough to be successful, so that I may be able to allow their souls to rest in peace."

Again as if replaying the dream around him, as they moved out onto the river she guided him as he steered the boat down the river hugging close to the riverside. Again, as they reached the point on the river where the large fallen pine reached out into the river below the sandstone bluff, Aymer raised her hand for him to slow the boat. Ah Bao wondered if it was because he was simply tired and experiencing some sort of deja vu, or if perhaps because of his knowledge of the river in his dream he had selected this place on the river as the most likely spot in bad weather for an accident. He threw out the small anchor, and with the net they again began the task that they had undertaken in his dream.

Over and over, he threw out his net, seined it in, and clearing its contents of whatever objects that had become trapped in its webbing. Each time they moved a little further down the river, and as the night progressed, Ah Bao began to be convinced that although he respected and sympathized with Aymer, they were engaged in a fruitless effort. He threw his net countless times as the moon rapidly seemed to slide across the sky reaching its apex, then inch its way back down again toward the horizon.

The dawn was rapidly approaching and as Ah Bao hauled in the net one more time he wondered what Aymer might do faced with the fact that she would not be able to succeed in her task. As if at that moment she too accepted the inevitable, that time was quickly running out, Aymer said, "It's time. We must return to the riverbank."

Ah Bao didn't answer, he was at a loss for words for what he might say to her, and merely turned, took up the oars and began rowing hard up the river toward where he secured his boat. Aymer sat in the back of the boat her head down, shoulders slumped, her whole body an expression of the feeling of defeat she must have been feeling.   As he rowed Ah Bao looking over his shoulder could begin to see the fog and mist above the eddies swirling over the hidden rocks and shoals below, and knew it was almost dawn.

As they reached the shore Ah Bao jumped from the boat just as it scraped the bottom, and taking the bow pulled with the momentum to drive it up onto the sandy bank. Aymer rose from the rear and stepped onto the sand and struggled to help Ah Bao beach the boat. As she did he looked across the bow of the boat at her and could see that her cheeks were soaked with tears. She stepped around the bow of the boat to stand in front of him. He was certain she was going to thank him, and he stopped her, embarrass that he hadn't been able to truly help her.

"What will you do now that the final day has passed for you to try and recover your family's remains? Is there anything else we can do?"

CHAPTER NINETEEN

Aymer stood in front of him and he could feel the warmth from her body. She had begun to sob silently. Not knowing what he was doing he wrapped her in his arms and pulled her toward him hoping to give her some element of comfort. He could think of nothing else to do to console her.

He wanted his show of concern to be an altruistic one but he could feel himself becoming aroused, the scent of her body intoxicating him. And at the same time it was as if he could feel the energy from his own body flowing into Aymer as it comforted her.

She looked up into his eyes and at that moment he would have given her anything she asked for.

"The moment the moon will become full and begin to wane doesn't occur until shortly after midnight tonight. Should you agree we would have a few more hours tonight when I could search. It's up to you."

"Certainly," Ah Bao said. He would have only asked that they stand together wrapped in each others arms for a few more minutes, but in the dizzying rapture for a brief second he closed his eyes and when he opened them again the sun had appeared and Aymer seemed to have dissolved in a mist just as the mist had lifted off of the river dissolving and disappearing.

He stood against his boat drained of all his energy, feeling like he might pass out, and he closed his eyes again drawing in a breath. Opening them, he saw the lovely gray fox it's tail and paws tipped in white sitting beside the saw grass looking back at him, its eyes shining. Then as if at some unheard signal it bounded off into the tall grass.

Ah Bao stood staring at the place where the fox had disappeared into the grass hoping it would reappear. After a few minutes he realized it wasn't going to return and he pushed himself away from the side of the boat. He felt slightly sick to his stomach and wanted only to get back up to his cottage and lay down for a little while. He wasn't sure he could make it back up the hill unassisted.

Slowly he trudged back up the steep slope through the trees to the road stopping to catch his breath at the top of the ridge. From where he stood he could see past the edge of the bamboo and into one corner of the courtyard. He was able to just catch a glimpse of a darkened sleeve of someone standing inside the courtyard. The old monk had returned.

Hurrying across the road he notice that he had begun to limp slightly and he massaged his left side just below his ribs where he had suddenly developed a stitch in his side which was causing his limp. He stumbled into the courtyard ready to greet the old monk but standing in front of him was his friend Lu Xin Jun. He wore his brown and khaki uniform, a broadsword at his side, an even broader smile on his face.

"Ah Bao, you're back. Where have you been out to so early? I came over expecting to find you at home but you were gone." Without waiting for an answer he had grabbed Ah Bao's shoulders and shook him hard overcome with excitement at seeing his friend again after so long.

Ah Bao too was overjoyed at seeing his best friend, and took him by the arm and led him over to the stone bench, needing to sit down. Slapping him on the shoulder, he said, "And so the conquering hero finally returns home, eh?" And getting a closer look at his friend in the morning sun he noticed an angry thin red scar running along his jaw line ending where it turned up under his chin. "And what's this? A battle scar?" Ah Bao pinched his friend's chin good naturedly.

"Oh that's nothing," Xin Jun answered in a self-effacing tone. "We had a run-in with some bandits up north this Spring. There's a warlord up there that still doesn't want to pay allegiance to the Republic. We had to show him who was boss. Our commander is straight as they come. All spit and polish, and unlike some does everything by the book."

Xin Jun stopped for a moment as if just now getting a good look at his friend for the first time and a worried look came over his face. He could see from the dark circles under his eyes, Ah Bao had aged in the year they had been separated. He was noticeably thinner too. "What has happened to you, old friend? It looks like you've been burning the candle at both ends." He stopped himself realizing his friend had a very good reason for the change in his appearance, and had forgotten that he had come over to pay his respects though he had not been exactly sure what he was going to say. He wanted to kick himself for putting his foot in his mouth.

"Ah Bao, I'm so sorry about your parents. I wish I could have been her to burn ming paper with you at their funeral."

"Thank you, brother, but there wasn't much of a funeral. Not that I wouldn't have liked for you to be here. But I really wasn't able to do as much as I would have liked to honor them." Ah Bao said this, and looked down at his hands, which he formed into fists, then relaxed them as he continued. "There was a real scare when influenza spread through the village. The mayor wouldn't allow anyone to hold more than a day's funeral before I was forced to bury my parents. They weren't the only ones who got sick but it just wasn't fair; it wasn't respectful the way everything was so hurried."

Ah Bao looked at his friend from head to foot and felt like a part of himself had been returned to him. They were two halves of a complimenting spirit and it was almost as if each could guess what the other one was thinking. Ah Bao was the thoughtful one, and Xin Jun spoke his mind without really thinking. Xin Jun spent his money easily, perhaps because of his family's situation, while Ah Bao was the frugal one. It wasn't as if they never argued, but when they did, they easily resolved their differences.

"You're right Xin Jun. The past year has really been a rough one, but the past several weeks have only added considerably to the... ordeal." Ah Bao knew his friend's take on what he had been recently experiencing would be diametrically different from what he himself thought and felt but he wanted to hear what his friend had to say.

"What is it friend? Tell me."

"Well, a couple of weeks ago I met a young woman."

"My young friend," Xin Jun always pointed out whenever he had the opportunity that he was several months older than Ah Bao. "How could that be a bad thing?" And a wide grin returned to his face.

"Well, it's more than that. I've been helping her during the last couple of weeks and that's where I was last night. The problem is, and this you're not going to believe, and this I'm almost certain; at the break of dawn, twice now, she's vanished, and a fox appeared in her place."

"What? You're not serious. You think she's a fox spirit?" Xin Jun stopped himself and grabbed Ah Bao's forearm hard, and after a long moment began tapping his finger against his own lips, looking as if trying to recall something. "You know me, Ah Bao, I'm not much of one for reading, but I remember seeing something in one of the books that Mei Mei left lying around a few years back.

"I remember reading that there have been these fox spirits have been talked about, whispered about, because you don't want people to think you're crazy, throughout our history. As I remember even thousands of years ago there was a man, I think his name was Huang Yuan who was led into a cave by a dog, but perhaps a fox, and found the cave inhabited by goddesses. I think he ended up marrying one of these goddesses. It's said that very often fox spirits are looking for a mate, or even for some kind of revenge.

"Are you sure you are awake when you meet this woman? And is she very beautiful?" Xin Jun didn't wait for an answer, caught up in relating what he knew, and continued. "Sometimes the fox spirit is the ghost of a human seeking a proper burial, say from a drowning. Or they try to lure a human to their death as a replacement for their own spirit. The fox spirit can't die, unless it is hunted by dogs and killed, but what is especially dangerous, and what humans must be careful of, is that when they come in contact with the fox spirit that it doesn't draw out their energy, their life essense, which the fox spirit needs to become more powerful and eventually become mortal again."

As Ah Bao listened to his friend explain what he knew, everything that had happened during the past month started to make sense. Even including the feeling he had experienced that morning when he had embraced Aymer and he had later felt so completely drained of his energy. He knew it wasn't simply he had worked so hard during the night or that he hadn't gotten enough sleep. It was much more than that. But given all this information he still couldn't deny his overpowering attraction for the woman.

"My god! What you're saying and what has been happening to me, together it is beginning to make complete sense. And what

I thought was my imagination you've read about, and as you say, it's nothing new." Ah Bao recalled how the monk had spoken to him, and although the old man had answered some of the doubts swimming in his brain, it had been more, perhaps what he would have called a philosophical explanation. His friend Xin Jun spoke in simple terms, and had shot straight to his heart. And yet, Ah Bao was convinced Aymer's motives were virtuous, he was committed to helping her, and he had a growing desire to find out more about her. He felt like he was being pulled in two directions. What was he to do?

"So, Ah Bao, I'm going to help you. Together we are going to trap this fox spirit. Then, with my sword if we can kill the fox it will stop tormenting you. When do you think you'll encounter this creature from another world, again?"

"Well, brother, I'm not quite sure," Ah Bao lied, alarmed at the thought that they might do Aymer, or the fox spirit she inhabited some harm. "It will probably be soon though," he added not wanting to tell his friend a bald-faced lie.

"Well, then. Get some rest, young brother. I have some things to do in the village. I'll see you later today or this evening, all right? But get some rest. You look terrible." Again, after he had spoken Xin Jun thought to himself that he should have tempered his words with a little discretion, but he was truly worried about his friend. Clapping Ah Bao on the shoulder Xin Jun jumped up and left the courtyard.

CHAPTER TWENTY

Ah Bao was relieved, yet confused. He was relieved at hearing Xin Jun's explanation which answered some of the questions about what had been happening to him, where he'd been during the past month, but Ah Bao was confused by his own tender feelings for Aymer, and Xin Jun's violent reaction toward her. Sitting in the warm morning sun, Ah Bao made the decision that he would avoid involving his friend in his dealings with Aymer, whatever they might be or become.

But in one respect his friend was right. He was completely exhausted and needed sleep badly. As he dragged himself into the cottage to lay down on the kang he realized he hadn't eaten since the previous morning but his exhaustion left him with no appetite at all except for sleep. Laying face down onto the kang he immediately asleep.

Ah Bao woke to a loud noise and although it seemed like only a few moments since he had closed his eyes from the warmth in the room he could tell it was much later in the day, perhaps around noon. Raising his head and turning toward the sound, he saw Mei Rong seated at the table looking at him expectantly.

"Shouldn't you be out fishing, big brother?" Mei Rong said, and Ah Bao could hear the reproach, the way a mother might say something to her small son. "Oh, that's right. You've found yourself a young woman, and you don't have time for fishing."

Ah Bao should have known that whatever he might say to Xin Jun would be information that would quickly shared with his sister. He didn't expect Mei Rong to take it the same way as her brother had, and she hadn't.

"So what, Ah Bao, are you two sweethearts lovers?" Lu Mei Rong seldom used Ah Bao's given name and when she did it was always in a tone of complete seriousness.

"Mei Mei, I just met the woman," Ah Bao said, though still lying on the kang and raising himself up on one elbow to answer her. "I hardly know her."

"Well, how do you feel about her, then? Xin Jun mentioned there was something, as he put it, unusual about her, but he wouldn't be any more specific than that."

"She's a woman in need of help, and I'm helping her. The other circumstances are really immaterial." Ah Bao knew he wasn't telling her the truth but he had seen how Xin Jun had reacted when he had been frank with him and imagined that Mei Rong might react as unpredictably.

"You still haven't said how you feel about her."

Sitting upright and throwing his legs over the side of the kang, he scratched the back of his neck and took a moment to answer Mei Rong. Then holding his hands up he said, as if offering an excuse, and a little defensive, "She's a lovely, sweet woman that I've met who needs help, which I can give. And yes, I'm attracted to her." Ah Bao wouldn't lie, or could he completely hide his feelings from someone with whom at times growing up together he had shared his innermost feelings, though at this moment he could see in Mei Rong's eyes the hurt she was feeling at hearing how he felt toward Aymer.

"Then Ah Bao," she answered, "I suggest you do what you need to do. You should know if you need someone to talk to, or anything, for that matter that I'll be here. You understand how I feel about you, don't you?" Mei Rong looked like she might be about to burst into tears, but she held her feelings in, and without waiting for an answer she looked down, brushed something unseen from the front of her dress, slowly rose, and left the cottage.

Sitting on the kang Ah Bao was left feeling even more confused. How could helping one person hurt another person as sweet and caring as Mei Rong? He had hoped that Mei Rong would see the altruistic nature of what he was doing. Ah Bao wasn't so naïve as to think that his feelings for Aymer wouldn't effect Mei Rong, but he hadn't considered that they might also excluded Mei Rong from his heart. And it wasn't only loyalty he felt for Mei Rong. Selfishly it was also her constancy in his life that he didn't want to lose.

Ah Bao sat on the edge of the kang deep in thought wondering what was happening to him. He wanted his life to be simply and the rules clear and easy to follow, and yet at each turn things became more difficult to understand. He was only raised from his thoughts by a gnawling hunger in his belly. He thought that he could smell something delicious, reminiscent of his mother's cooking, the ginger, garlic, and soy, and wondering if he was imagining it. Then looking over at the table he saw that Mei Rong must have brought a plate of food and left it under a small embroidered towel in the center of the table.

On wobbly legs he walked over to the table and sat down. With both hands he carefully lifted the cloth, embroidered with large red camelias, and tiny swallows that he recognized as Mei Rong's handiwork, revealing the dishes beneath. Lifting the cover revealed a small round mountain of rice, and on one side of the rice were sauted garlic sprouts with a few slivers of browned chicken, and on the other side, a helping of mapo dofu, the shiny pieces of dofu arranged in rows in the glistening spicy chili sauce. Ah Bao couldn't help thinking that the plate looked like a lovely landscape, the ginger sprouts, a tiny green crop, and the mapo dofu perhaps a freshly cultivated rice paddy nestled against the tiny mountain.

Unable to control his hunger he began to devour the lovely scene in front of him.
Although there were subtle differences in the tastes and ingredients in the dishes, as he savored the food Ah Bao allowed himself to be lost in the thought that his mother had just made the dishes for him and was still alive.

CHAPTER TWENTY-ONE

Lost in this reverie he didn't hear the monk enter the courtyard and it was only that the old monk had stopped in the doorway, blocking the light that brought Ah Bao back to reality.

"May I come in and sit down?" The monk asked.

"Oh, old brother, you've come. I should have been expecting you. Have you eaten?"

"Yes, I ate my meal at the temple."

"Well, then let me at least offer you some tea." Ah Bao rose from the table and moving to the long table against the wall picked up the teapot which sat on one corner, and turned it over to fill a cup. The teapot was empty except for a few drops of stale tea.

Seeing this, the monk said, "A cup of clear water would be more than enough."

Ah Bao scurried over to the cook stove where the fresh water stood in the pail and ladled out a bowlful for the old monk. He was embarassed at not having any tea to offer the old monk but was overflowing with emotion at having another guest in his home. It seemed he had more guests in this one day than during most of the preceding year.

Carrying the water over and setting it down in front of the monk Ah Bao abandoned his food and began relating what had happened to him since the previous day when they had been together. The old monk listened quietly until Ah Bao got to the part where his friend Xin Jun had volunteered to help him. The monk shook his head, and Ah Bao guessed that he had something to say, and stopped speaking.

"The Dao De Jing will tell you, weapons are instruments of fear," the monk said. "They are not a wise man's tools. But please continue."

Ah Bao wondered to himself if this meant he was right in avoiding Xin Jun's help or if it meant that he should allow Xin Jun to help but he needed to insist that his friend abandon his sword if he was to help him in completing his task. But Ah Bao decided to think more on that later and see what he had to say about the rest of his problems.

He continued to explain what had happened after Xin Jun had left, he had fallen asleep, and Mei Rong had come over to bring him food, and speak to him. The old monk sat and slowly stroked his beard as Ah Bao related what had happened. Ah Bao told him how he had seen how much it had bothered Mei Rong to hear that that he was attracted to Aymer, but he felt he had to tell her. Now, he was hoping the monk would have an easy answer for him to follow. When he had finished, the monk spoke.

"One who knows others is intelligent; one who understands himself is enlightened," the monk said. "One who conquers others is powerful, but one who is able to control himself is mighty. This might seem rather nebulous to you but I will say simply that for you to figure out your problems with Mei Rong you must first understand and control your own feelings. This is as simple as it gets."

This was not what Ah Bao was expecting to hear. He had expected the monk to tell him something he should do, or could say to Mei Rong, to make things right. He wasn't comfortable with simply wrestling through the problem on his own and coming to terms with whatever he must come to terms with in himself.

"But I can see you are tired from talking and haven't fully recuperated from your experience this morning." The monk said. "Let me show you some movements to help refresh your body and your spirit." At this the old monk stood up, took Ah Bao by the arm and led him over to the western side of the courtyard to a wide shady area.

The monk began with the simplest movements of tai chi, raising his hands and showing the movements, and instructing Ah Bao when to breath in, and when to breath out. The movements followed those of the primordial animals, the bird, the horse, the monkey, the tiger and the snake, and as Ah Bao followed trying to imitate the movements the monk showed him he forgot completely about the problems he had been experienced and concentrated solely on the moment.

The grasped the bird's tail, and tried to feel the energy, the qi that he was encompassing. He moved his hands like clouds, he carried the tiger, he separated the horses mane. When he completed these moves the old monk showed him where he was making mistakes and guided him in the proper form. When they were finished Ah Bao's drained spirit and body felt truly refreshed.

"Do you feel the softness in your body where you were hard before?" The old monk asked smiling. "Do your problems seem not quite so overwhelming now?"

"Yes, old brother. Thank you. And I want to learn more. It's strange how it makes me feel wonderfully alive."

"Not really so strange," the monk said. "You are moving the qi through your body on the different meridians, cleansing, and energizing your body."

Tai chi When a man is living he is tender and fragile. When he dies he is hard and stiff.

As he is leaving the monk said, "When one recognizes the presence of Dao he understands where to stop. Knowing where to stop he is free from danger. Courage carried to daring leads to death. Courage restrained by caution leads to life. Of these two cases the one appears to be advantageous, and the other to be injurious."

CHAPTER TWENTY-TWO

Ah Bao fell asleep after the monk left, and sleeping until dusk, woke, and as in the dream he met Aymer at the river, and together they put the boat in the water. It was already dark by the time they had reached the middle of the river and the moon hadn't come out. Ah Bao could only just see the outline of Aymer's face as he steered the boat into more rapid shoals of the river.

The moon had just come up when Aymer whispered "Please, Ah Bao, over by that cliff. Can we look over there."

Ah Bao knew the cliff she was talking about, as they approached it from the right, and he knew he would need to fight the current to turn the boat, and come to settle against the cliff without breaking the boat against the cliff. Ah Bao had fished it many times with his father, and they had always caught fish there.

Ah Bao managed to easily turn the boat in the current, and pulled up the small sail the boat had to change directions, and with the wind coming up the channel managed to slow the boat, as he threw out his anchor, and gently come to rest against the granite rock that formed the face of the cliff. The water beneath the cliff was inky black, reflecting only the moon.

Ah Bao picked up his net and heaved it into the current allowing the net to be carried away from the side of the boat. He waited until he thought the weights had reached the bottom of the river, Aymer watching him, her hands tightly gripping the rails of the boat, as if expecting something. But when he pull in the net, gathering the purse, as the water emptied from it, the net was completely empty, and he threw it out again, this time further up the side of the boat. And, again when he pulled it in, it was empty.

Then finally, throwing his net for a third time, letting it settle while he rested a minute, his back and arms still throbbing with effort. As he began to pull the net in one more time, Ah Bao felt an astonishingly heavy weight against it, an ominously dead weight, unlike any he had felt on the previously nights.

As he slowly seined in the net, pursing it together to trap the contents that were held within it, weighing heavily against the belly of the net he could see what appeared on the water's surface, in the half-darkness, to be a drifting bolt of torn cloth. Aymer let out a cry, a long, woeful sound, and stumbled forward in the boat toward him where he crouched in the bow, almost capsizing it. "Careful, Aymer. You'll turn the boat over," Ah Bao said sternly, then tempered his tone with kindness. "Please, we don't want to wind up in the river," he said softly.

"My mother," Aymer cried in an aching whisper, and kneeling beside him, helped Ah Bao gently raise the weight of the net into the boat.

As Aymer tenderly lay the net and its contents down against the wooden hull of the boat, Ah Bao could see the cloth more clearly, and now he could easily recognize it was a long, tattered dress, and what were no more than bones, stripped clean by the fish, held together by only a few strings of sinews. Though he felt a slight revulsion at touching them, he helped Aymer extract the bones carefully from the netting. "Please, I think we should move further down river." she whispered.

Again they began the process of working their way down the river, turning and slowly their progress, repeatedly throwing out the net and gathering it in, Ah Bao was finding some untapped energy, spurred on by Aymer's urgency. After numerous more tries, another weight bellied the net, and they recovered another smaller string of bones swathed in clothes. Aymer said they were those of her brother. Then finally, a much heavier burden dragged at the net, and they recovered the bones of her father.

Looking up at him, a sad smile parting Aymer's lips, tears beginning to well in her eyes, and a sense of relief filled her face. Her voice trembling, she said, "Thank you. Thank you, for each of my family. Thank you so very much. And now, Mr. Ah Bao, I must go ashore and bury my family."

Ah Bao lifted the anchor and pulled at the oars, the sail useless, the wind having died down as dawn approached. As they moved back up the river, Aymer pointed to a spot not far from where Ah Bao had first seen her, where he sunned his boat on the beach, and down the hill from his home. Ah Bao brought the boat up next to where Aymer had pointed, a sheltering bend in the river, where he could beach his boat.   As the boat reached the beach Aymer jumped ashore, and hurried up the riverbank, disappearing among the tall rushes that lined the bank. After a few moments she returned, hurrying back down the beach. Aymer gently gathered up the bones of her brother in her arms, and again headed back up the beach and through the rushes in the direction she had come. Looking after her, Ah Bao tried to convince himself to pick up the bones of the mother, but found himself frozen where he sat, a strange chill on the back of his neck. After a few moments, Aymer returned, and lovingly gathered the bones of her mother in her arms and moved off again through rushes. He waited looking down at the last pile of cloth and bones until she returned. Returning, and bending down she tried to take up the bones of her father in her arms, tired as she was, it seemed to much for her. She tried again, and Ah Bao gritted his teeth, and slid his arms under the leg bones that protruded from the tattered black pant legs, and together they moved up the riverbank. Aymer pushed her way through the rushes and they came out into a large uneven grassy field. Carefully stepping across the swales and rises of the uneven ground of the field, they reached an area of young willows and locust trees, and laid the bones of her father next to other two smaller piles of bones of her mother and little brother.

Then unfolding the tattered fold of her father's pants took out a small leather bag, wet and shiny as a shark's skin. Aymer handed the bag to Ah Bao, and said, "Here is the gold I promised you and I want you to have."

Ah Bao took the small, wet bag from her hands, the bag unusually heavy, and pushed it deep down into his own pocket. The bag pressed heavy against his leg. He didn't know what to say to Aymer. All his wishes had been granted, and all he could think to say was, "Thank you."

Turning away from Ah Bao, Aymer began digging furiously with her hands in the loose earth where one of the swales rose up beneath the canopy of the trees. He realized she was digging the graves for her family, and he fell on his knees beside her and began working with her to clear a shallow depression in the earth. Watching her as she dug, Ah Bao could see that her fingers soon began to bleed, but she continued to scratch at the dirt, pulling small handfuls of the more compact dirt out and toward the sides of the depression.

 Ah Bao thought to himself, although he hadn't known Aymer's family, how tragic the family's death was, yet, how fortunate they were to have a daughter whose filial love for them was boundless. The thought filled his mind, and he dug all the harder alongside her, his callused hands more able to withstand the rough soil.

Finally, when she seemed satisfied with the grave, together they laid the bones of the three bodies, side by side, within the small depression and gathered armloads of the soil pushing it down over them. After carefully, lovingly patting the soil smoothly across the grave, Aymer took from a fold of her gown a thick pack of golden funeral money. With a match she lit several leafs of paper, and laid them on the ground beside the grave. Then separating the rest of the money she fed the small pile of paper into the fire. Having completed this task, she rose from the side of the grave, and with Ah Bao following her, Aymer made her way back down to the riverside.

From the sleeve of her gown she withdrew three small pressed paper boats and gentle unfolded them. She delicately placed each on the surface of the water, and watched as each floated out on slowly into the current, then more quickly caught up in the swifter water, and carried, disappearing down the river. Turning to Ah Bao, she looked up into the brightening sky, and said, "I have succeeded, Mr. Chen Wen Ming. Their spirits are now at rest. It's been only with your help, I've been able to do this."

CHAPTER TWENTY-THREE

Aymer's eyes again turned to the eastern horizon, Ah Bao's eyes followed, and they both saw that the light of the morning was approaching. "How will I ever be able to thank you?" she asked.

Then as he looked deep into her eyes, he was lost for a moment in their loveliness, and then the sadness seemed to rise from within her. Aymer took each of his hands in her own and kissed them gently, and as she did he felt hot tears falling onto the backs of his hands. The soft warmth of her lips on his skin, and the wetness of her tears like a gentle flame ignited a fire of its own within him, and as she raised her face from his hands, and as if again in a dream, he gently pulled her toward him. Her body seemed to melt against his, their lips touching fusing together in a moment of intoxicating warmth.

His whole being, his arms, his legs, every muscle in his body seemed to thirst for her. Then still holding his hands, she took a step away from him, holding him at arm's length, Aymer moved slowly into the water. Following, he stepped into the water beside her, and together they moved slowly out against the sheltering bend of the river.

Standing together waist deep in the cool water they kissed again, and a passionate fire melded her to him. The light in the Eastern sky was brightening, and together they slowly sank below the surface of the water, their prolonged kiss seeming to pull the very essence of his being into hers, and he felt a longing, a desire for her beauty, her tenderness, her sweet gentle love, and he wished only that their kiss would never end.

Ah Bao could feel the warmth of Aymer's legs and could feel her breasts as she floated against him, the cool water eddied around them, the steady pull of the river drawing them out into its currents. He could sense that the currents were drawing the a little out into the more dangerous currents of the river, but he didn't care. As they wrapped their arms around each other not wanting to be pulled apart by the currents, there was something that told him if he could simply hold her close to him, if he could keep the river from separating them, than they could be together, and she wouldn't be lost to him.

The warmth and pressure of her body seemed to draw him even closer to the essence of her own being. He felt giddy from lack of air but he tried not to care, wanting only to hold her to him, feel her against him, and not allow the waters to take her from him. He knew it would take every ounce of strength that he still possessed, every part of him, both body and soul, to keep them from being separated as the river moved them out into its currents, intoxicating into the depths of its channel.

It was the soft pressure of her body, and the warmth of her embrace that were like sparks between them, that held him to her. Still, as they floated out into the channel, feet below the surface, the heavy bag of gold helping to hold him down, Ah Bao continued to think how much Aymer had sacrificed herself to save her family. Recalling the sadness he had seen in Aymer's eyes, when she had first told him of losing her family, swept through him like a wave.

Ah Bao thought about his own family, his own mother now gone a year, and the passing, a little more than a the year before, of his father. Suddenly, he was struck by his own selfishness, and knew that he was doing something terribly wrong. Although he wanted Aymer more than anything, to hold her like this pressed against him in this loving embrace, he asked himself how could he give up his own life, forsake himself like this, giving up the precious lifeblood which his parents had given him?

He knew he wanted to allow himself to be drawn with Aymer down into the depths of the river. Still, the sweet embrace of her arms around him, holding him, as if swaddled in some heavenly flower, and the weight of the bag in his pocket kept him from rising to the surface of the river. He wanted to rise, but his body felt as if it was wrapped in the countless petals of a warm, lovely, lotus flower. His lungs began to burn for air, yet her touch was the most pleasurable sensation he had ever experienced.

He couldn't let go, he didn't want to let go of her, and yet his mind, his subconscious kept reminding him he had to survive, he must not let her draw him any deeper into the depths of the river. For a long moment, they were carried further along on the currents together, Ah Bao knowing that he must break away. But at the instant when he told himself to released her, he found himself gripping her to even tighter, with all his strength, his mind crying out to release her, though his heart simply wanting only to feel their bones meld together as one.

And then, at what must have been the last possible instant, his brain not allowing him to do otherwise, he gently pushed himself away from Aymer, and clawed for the surface of the river. His lungs felt like empty vacuums, and he was convinced he wouldn't make it to the surface, though he knew, if he didn't, he would suck the water of the river into his lungs, and die.

CHAPTER TWENTY-FOUR

He may have lost complete consciousness for a second, but the force of his struggle propelled him toward the surface. He wasn't sure if he had taken the weight of the gold from his pocket, and dropped it, to let him reach the surface quicker, he knew he had considered it, but just as he could no longer control the primordial desire to open his mouth, and inhale the water of the river, his head bobbed above the surface and the morning air flooded his lungs.

He was far down the river from where his boat had beached itself, and the currents continued with each passing moment to carry him further down the river, toward the swifter rapids which he knew he hadn't the strength, or the conviction, to fight against. Ah Bao knew he was at a crossroads, and he told himself if he was going to survive, to stroke sideways against the currents, and he managed, miraculously, to reach an area of calm, resting his feet against the sandy bottom. His legs gave way beneath him as he tried to walk through the water toward the shore. He half swam, half stumbled closer to shore, and as he came out of the water and stood, his whole body trembled, and he fell to his knees.

Resting near the shore, gasping for breath, the morning sun broke above the ridge behind him and slowly he could feel its rays begin to warm his back, and he wept. He wept for his passionate insanity, he wept from relief, but most of all he wept for the love he knew he had lost.

Looking up, where he knelt in the water, his eyes blurred with tears, for an instant on the rise of the riverbank above him, through the brush, he thought he saw a long, gray-brown fox crouching, watching him. Then, when he had risen to stand on unsteady legs, he looked at the same place, and whatever he had seen was gone.

Standing up he could feel that he still had the weight of the bag of gold in his pocket, and knew he must take it and hide it somewhere that thieves couldn't find it. Ah Bao took the gold home to his cottage and dug out a brick from the wall underneath his parents photographs, and place the gold beneath it, and replaced the brick.

Ah Bao, at least during this life, never saw Aymer again. He took to going out more days on the river with his boat, fishing the spots his father had fished. Some days his catch was quite large, and he began to acquire a little wealthy.

After several years of living in solitude, a matchmaker strengthened her resolve to make a match for Ah Bao with Mei Rong, and in the prescribed amount of time, they were married. She gave him three lovely children, two of them mei meis of her own, and Ah Bao took his son, and sometimes his daughters out on the boat to fish, and learn the water. Ah Bao and Mei Rong shared a marriage, at times passionate, and happy, as happily as many marriages are. And mostly, they spent their love on their children.

Yet, Ah Bao never completely forgot the lovely Aymer, and the night they had spent on the river. Ah Bao would go fishing each day laying his nets, gathering his catch, and selling his fish at the market. Then, there were the rare days he might look up from his nets, and see a lovely Grey-brown fox sitting in the tall grass on the riverbank watching him. Ah Bao's eyes, for a long moment, would meet the bright, shining eyes of the fox, and he'd feel a warm glow. Then, there had been a couple of times when he had stayed out fishing past dusk, and he convinced himself for an instant he had seen Aymer, a faint image of a young woman standing far away along the riverbank, where he had seen a fox, a moment before, in the dusk. Then each time as it got darker, he had convinced himself he had been wrong.

Afterwards
, on other days, recalling to himself what he thought he had seen, his eyes might burn a little, water unnaturally, like from dust, or perhaps, he thought, because of the brisk breeze blowing across the surface of the river, and he might feel a moistness on his cheeks, too. But he would smile because he knew that, all in all, life had been good to him, and as he got older, he realized that in his life he had been truly blessed.